A Thief on Morgan's Plantation

By Lisa Banim

Illustrated by
Tatyana Yuditskaya

SILVER MOON PRESS
NEW YORK

First Silver Moon Press Edition 1995

Copyright © 1995 by Lisa Banim
Illustration copyright © 1995 by Tatyana Yuditskaya

For information write:

Silver Moon Press
New York, NY
(800) 874-3320

Library of Congress Cataloging-in-Publication Data

Banim, Lisa, 1960–
A Thief on Morgan's Plantation / by Lisa Banim;
Illustrated by Tatyana Yuditskaya.—1st Silver Moon Press ed.
p.   cm. — (Mysteries in time)
Summary: After being sent to live on her uncle's plantation in
Maryland at the start of the Civil War, Constance Morgan finds herself
defending a slave child accused of stealing a family heirloom.
ISBN 1-881889-62-9: $14.95
1. Maryland—History—Civil War, 1861–1865—Juvenile fiction.
[1. United States—History—Civil War, 1861–1865—Fiction.
2. Maryland—Fiction 3. Slavery—Fiction] I. Yuditskaya, Tatyana, ill.
II. Title III. Series
PZ7.B2253Th   1994
[Fic]—dc20
94-34961
CIP
AC

10 9 8 7 6 5 4

Printed in the USA

To Peter, Kim, Stephanie, and Rory, with love
L.B.

To the memory of Allen Barber, teacher and artist
T.Y.

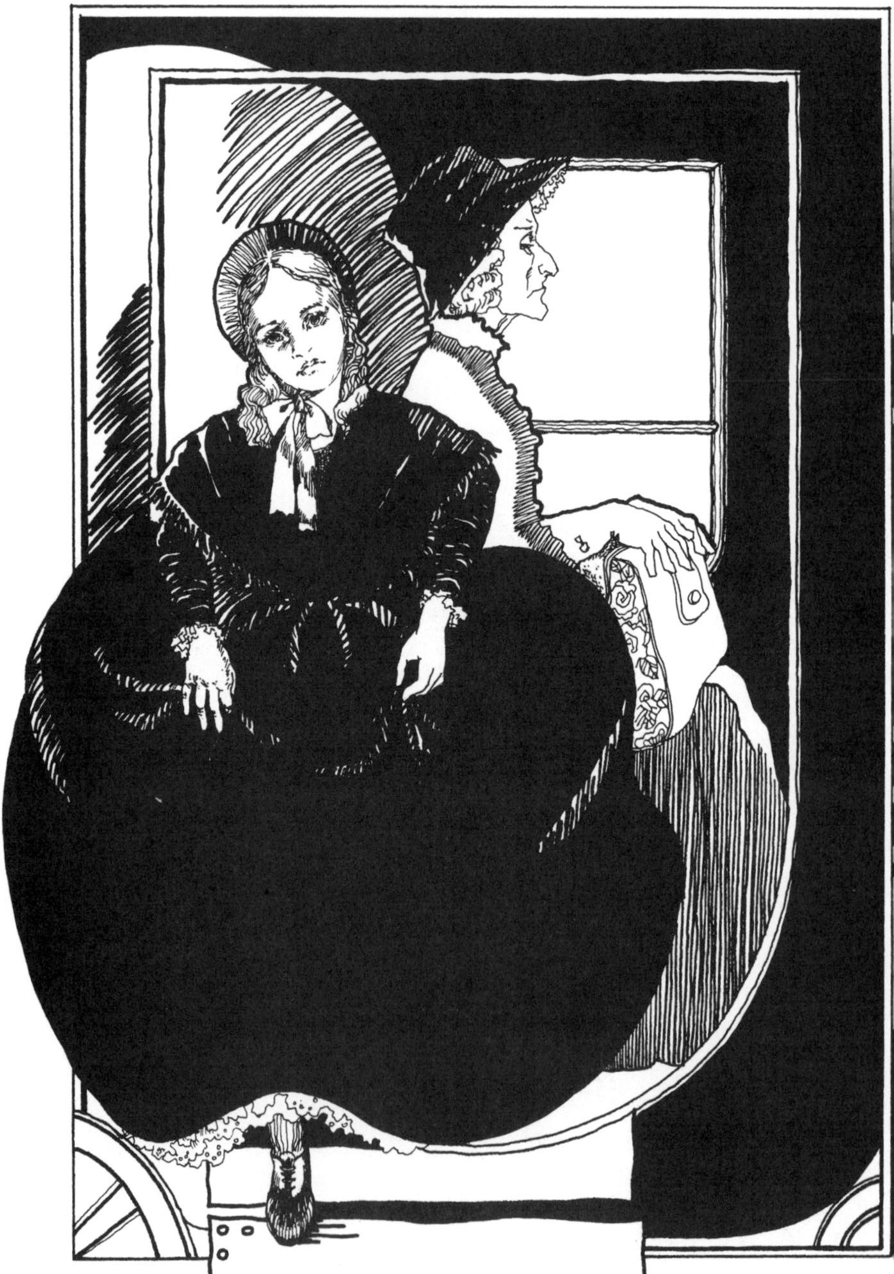

1

Eleven-year-old Constance Morgan leaned closer to the dusty carriage window, and tried to catch a breath of fresh air. It was stifling hot inside the coach, even on this mid-April morning in 1861.

"Sit back, Constance," the woman beside her said sharply. "You don't want to be seen looking anxious. It isn't becoming for a young lady."

Constance slumped back in her seat. "Yes, Miss Finch," she said.

"Surely you want to make a good impression on your uncle and his family," Miss Finch went on. "Mr. Tobias Morgan is an important man down here in Maryland."

Constance sighed. "Yes, Miss Finch," she said again. She wanted to remind Miss Finch that her own father was an important man, too, back in Philadelphia. Or rather, he had been, until he'd lost his fortune on a risky business deal.

But he is going to earn all that money back,

1

Constance told herself. After all, that was why her father went out west to pan for gold on Pikes Peak, Colorado. So far, he hadn't had much luck, but he was determined to stay and build a whole new life for the two of them.

Once he struck it rich, he would send for her. But right now, she was making the journey south from Philadelphia to stay with her father's brother, Uncle Tobias, and his family. She had never met them, even though they were her only living relations.

"Please tell me about my cousins again," Constance asked Miss Finch. "I want to know every-thing about them."

Miss Finch sniffed impatiently. "There is nothing more to tell," she said. "According to your father's let-ter, Miss Melanie is around your age. And there is a boy as well, I believe."

By the pinched look on Miss Finch's pale face, Constance could tell that her companion did not think much of boys. In fact, Miss Finch did not think much of children in general. She had kept house for Constance and her father for three years, ever since Constance's mother had died, but Constance had never been fond of her sharp-tongued chaperone. Constance was glad she was going to live with Uncle Tobias and his family for a while. Anything would be better than staying alone with Miss Finch.

"Adjust your bonnet, Constance," Miss Finch said. "The ribbons are dangling, and you look most untidy."

Constance pushed back the small gray bonnet over her light brown hair and smoothed the folds of her gray wool dress. The wool was making her itchy, even through her petticoats, and she felt warmer than ever. But Miss Finch felt strongly that Constance should wear sober clothes in mourning for her mother.

Mother wouldn't like to see me wearing these drab dresses, Constance told herself. She had a feeling that Miss Finch was simply too lazy to make her new clothes. The carriage jolted when the wheels hit a large stone in the dirt road.

"Easy, driver!" Miss Finch called to the front of the carriage. "Pay attention!"

"Yes, ma'am," the driver said with a tip of his hat.

Miss Finch fanned herself with the black lace fan she had taken out of her small flowered carpetbag. "We're just outside Baltimore now," she said. "It should not be much farther to Mr. Morgan's plantation."

Constance stole another peek out the carriage window as soon as Miss Finch's head was turned. She couldn't see very well, since the window was covered with dust and dried mud, but she could make out huge green fields that stretched far into the distance. *Tobacco,* Constance thought. That's what her father had said Uncle Tobias and many of the other landowners in Maryland grew on their enormous plantations.

Suddenly, a man on horseback thundered past the carriage. This kicked up another great cloud of dust.

Constance coughed, and Miss Finch covered her face with a handkerchief. "We're nearly there, I'm sure," Miss Finch said. "Do stop sputtering, or your eyes will be all red and watery. It would be most unattractive."

A few minutes later, the carriage rumbled through an open gate and up a long, gently sloping hill. It came to a stop just in front of the flagstone steps that led to an imposing white house with a porch and white columns. Constance could feel her heart beating faster.

"Really, Constance," Miss Finch scolded. "Your mouth is hanging open like a donkey's. Close it at once, if you please. It's time for you to get out of this dreadful carriage. Remember to look after yourself and mind your p's and q's."

Constance turned to her companion in surprise. "Aren't you going in, too? Won't you be staying for a while to recover from the journey?"

Miss Finch waved a hand. "Good heavens, no," she said. "I will return to Philadelphia at once. I have a new position awaiting me there."

"Oh," Constance said. Even though she had just been eager to be rid of the awful Miss Finch, suddenly she didn't feel very happy about it. She was about to enter a house full of strangers, even if they were her relations, and she would have to live there until her father sent for her. Who knew how long that would take?

The carriage door swung open. "Watch your step,

4

Miss," the perspiring driver said.

Quickly, Constance gathered her skirts and stepped over Miss Finch's ugly black shoes. "Good-bye," she told the woman breathlessly.

Miss Finch gave a curt nod. "Good-bye, Miss Morgan," she said briskly. "Judging from the look of this fancy house, I'm sure your relations will treat you well."

The driver grasped Constance by the waist and swung her down to the ground. "There you go, Miss," he said. "Your trunks are over there at the bottom of the steps."

Constance nodded as the driver took his place at the front of the carriage and picked up the reins. "Git," he told the horses.

Even before Constance could raise her hand to wave, the carriage pulled away in still another cloud of dust.

Blinking in the bright sunshine, Constance watched the carriage disappear down the long drive. She felt lost and lonely, and her legs seemed wobbly beneath her, as though she were still in the carriage.

The green fields that surrounded her were absolutely still. She gazed up at the huge, forbidding house and shuddered. What would her new life be like?

And why hadn't anyone come out to meet her?

2

Constance stood frozen at the bottom of the steps, still gazing wide-eyed at Uncle Tobias's stately house. Should she go inside, or should she wait for someone to notice her? And what would she do with her steamer trunks?

Suddenly, one of the top-floor windows was pushed up, and a black woman leaned out. Her hair was tied up in a dark blue kerchief.

"Lordy!" Constance heard the woman say. "It's that little Yankee girl, here already."

Already? Constance thought as the window closed again. It had seemed as though the three-day trip from Pennsylvania to Maryland had taken years.

A few moments later, two tall men came around the side of the house and picked up Constance's trunks. At almost the same time, the front doors of the great house opened and a boy with red hair and freckles came bounding down the steps.

"Hullo there!" the boy said. "I'm Toby, your

cousin." He took Constance's hand and shook it hard.

Constance drew back, a bit startled by the boy's friendliness. "My name is Constance," she said primly. Then, not wanting to sound too stuffy, she added, "It is very nice to meet you."

Toby squinted at her. "You don't look much like our part of the family," he said. "Wait until you see the old painting hanging in our parlor. My father and your father could be twins."

"People say I take after my mother," Constance said, looking at the ground. She wished that her mother could be here with her in this strange place.

Just then, the woman Constance had seen in the window came bustling down the steps. "Miss Constance!" she said breathlessly. "We weren't expecting you to arrive for another two days. Come right into the house this minute."

"Hattie is nursemaid to Melanie and me," Toby said to Constance as they started up the steps. "She used to take care of Wood, too, but he's too old for a nurse now."

"Wood?" Constance asked, frowning. Miss Finch had only mentioned two cousins. She couldn't recall her father saying anything about him, either.

"Oh, Wood's not around much," Toby said. "He's usually off in the fields with Father, or in town with his friends. You'll meet him later. But Melanie's inside."

Constance nodded. She couldn't wait to meet Melanie. She hoped they would be good friends.

When Constance stepped through the front doorway, she caught her breath in awe. Uncle Tobias's house was so much grander than the one her father owned — or used to own — back in Philadelphia. She looked around at the high ceilings, the ornate furniture, the floors covered with carpets from the Orient, and the wide mahogany staircase at the end of the hall. In one of the large rooms near the stairs, two young women were busily setting a long, shining table. In the middle of the table were two sets of elaborate silver candlesticks and a large bowl of fruit.

Toby tapped Constance on the shoulder. "Do you want to meet Melanie now? She's upstairs in her room most likely, primping in front of her mirror."

Hattie shooed him away. "Run along now, Master Toby. There'll be time enough for the girls to get to know each other later. This young lady must be bone tired."

She gave Constance a little push toward the stairs. "Come with me, child. Your room is just at the top here, right next to Miss Melanie's."

Constance trudged up the stairs after Hattie. The nursemaid was right. She was feeling very tired all of a sudden.

As she passed the dour-looking family portraits hanging on the wall, she felt goose bumps rising on her skin. All those stern old people seemed to be staring straight at her. *Yankee,* they were probably thinking.

Stop that! Constance scolded herself. No matter what happened between the Union and the Confederacy, she was sure her relations would be kind to her. Maryland had not seceded, or separated, from the Union, although many of the people who lived there thought that it should. Besides, Constance reminded herself, she was the Morgans' flesh and blood. Even if the tension between the two sides continued, no one would hold anything against an eleven-year-old relation. Or so Miss Finch had promised her.

Secretly, Constance wondered what her father would have said. Months ago, when he had suggested she stay with her relatives in Maryland, the nation was still a whole country. But two months before she left Philadelphia, back in February, six states — Georgia, Mississippi, Alabama, Louisiana, Florida, and Texas — had joined South Carolina in seceding from the Union. The seven states had formed the Confederate States of America. They'd even chosen their own president, Jefferson Davis of Mississippi, and written their own constitution. The seceded states felt that their individual rights were more important than the nation as a whole. They especially believed in their right to maintain slavery.

Constance's father, like many Americans on both sides, had hoped that there would be no war, that President Lincoln would be able to hold the Union together. But just a few days ago, on April 12, Confederate forces had fired on Fort Sumter. No one was killed on either side, but the Union soldiers had been forced to surrender the fort. Now it looked as though the problems between the states could not be solved without a war. The country had been torn in two.

"Here you are, Miss Constance," Hattie said, breaking into Constance's thoughts. "We have this room all fixed up for you. It's small, but right pretty."

Constance stepped into a bright, sunny room with slightly faded rose wallpaper. The curtains were light and sheer, and the white brass bed in the corner was covered with a colorful quilt. Constance's trunks were already set near the foot of the bed.

"I'll get you unpacked right away," Hattie said. "Now where are your trunk keys?"

Slowly, Constance pulled the keys from her dress pocket. She wasn't sure what to say. She had never had someone do things for her like this, except — rarely — Miss Finch. But that was different. Miss Finch was paid for her work. And she could leave her job whenever she wanted. She wasn't a slave, like Hattie.

Constance didn't know very much about slavery. Up north, it was against the law. In Philadelphia, all black people were free. Down south, most of them were slaves. Their owners believed that slavery was necessary to keep their plantations running. They claimed that they couldn't afford to pay workers high wages for long, difficult labor. Many people in the

North, like Constance's father, did not believe that black men, women, and children should be owned by anyone. Slavery was one of the issues about which the North and the South disagreed so bitterly.

"Lie right down on that bed," Hattie instructed Constance. "You want to be fresh and rested for noonday dinner."

Constance did as she was told, and the nursemaid went over to the door. "Ezra!" she called out into the hallway. "Come in here. I need you to fill a pitcher with fresh water from the well for Miss Constance. She'll need to wash up before dinner."

Constance opened one eye to see a boy about eight years old come into the room and take a painted porcelain pitcher from the washstand in the corner. Constance smiled at him shyly as Hattie steered him toward the door. "Now move along!" Hattie told him.

"Yes, Mama," Ezra said. The heavy pitcher seemed to overwhelm his small hands and arms.

As he hurried out with the empty pitcher, he nearly ran into a tall girl about Constance's age standing in the doorway. With her long, golden hair swept up in a lavender ribbon that matched her dress and her deep blue eyes, she was the prettiest girl Constance had ever seen.

"Mind where you're going," the girl said angrily, stepping back. "If you spill any water on my silk dress, I'll have you whipped for sure."

As Constance stared at the girl in surprise, Ezra

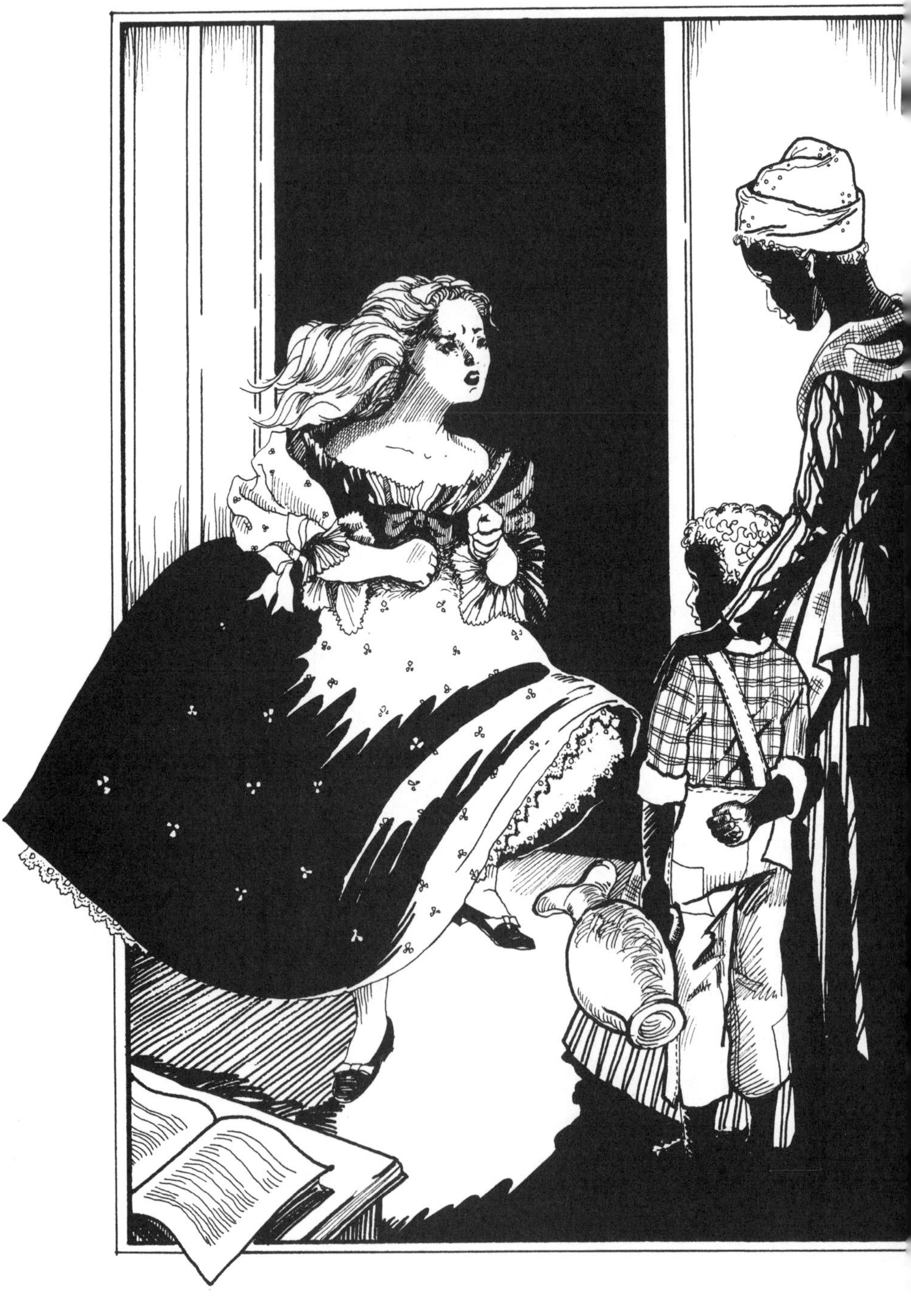

mumbled an apology and stepped past her out of the room.

"Now don't get yourself into a fit, Miss Melanie," Hattie told the blond girl. "I sent him running to fetch water for Miss Constance."

So that's Melanie! Constance thought. *Of course.* But her cousin certainly didn't seem very friendly.

Melanie swept into the room, her silk dress rustling. "There's no damage done, I suppose," she said to Hattie. "Not this time, anyway. But that boy of yours is very badly behaved." Suddenly, the girl seemed to notice Constance. "I'm Melanie," she said in a haughty tone. "You must be Cousin Constance."

"Hello," Constance said, scrambling off the bed. She could feel Melanie looking her up and down. "I'm Constance."

"Pleased to meet you, I'm sure," Melanie drawled. She glanced over at the trunks, which Hattie had opened and was now busily emptying. "You have only two?"

Constance nodded. "My old housekeeper, Miss Finch, said it was two trunks too many for a young girl."

Melanie gave a short laugh. "I suppose you Yankees are very thrifty. And overly fond of black," she added, nodding toward the dark-colored dresses spread out on the quilt.

Constance felt her face grow hot. Cousin Melanie was the rudest girl she had ever met! But she bit back the retort that was on the tip of her tongue. She didn't want to start off on the wrong foot with any of the Morgans.

Just then, Melanie's gaze fell upon a book lying open on the night stand, and she gave a shrill cry. "Why, whatever is this doing here?" she said, rushing over and snatching up the book. "It's mine!"

Constance shrank back. She hadn't even noticed the book earlier. But it wouldn't surprise her if Melanie blamed her for taking it.

Melanie looked from Hattie to Constance. Then her eyes narrowed. "It's that little sneak Ezra again," she said. "He stole it from my room!"

"He was just taking a peek at those fine pictures, most likely," Hattie said. "You won't catch him doing it again."

"See that he doesn't," Melanie said with a sniff. Then she turned and stalked out of the room.

Constance sank back down on the bed, stunned. Cousin Melanie was a horrible snob. And mean, too. How could Constance ever have thought the two of them could be like sisters?

Coming to stay with the Morgans was a terrible mistake, Constance thought miserably. She wanted to go back home to Philadelphia straight-away.

But it was too late now. Constance could only hope her father would come to get her soon.

3

Constance sat forlorn on the bed, tears in her eyes. Everyone, it seemed, had left her all alone.

Her mother had died and gone up to heaven. Her father had left her behind when he went out west to seek his fortune. Miss Finch had gotten rid of her at the earliest possible opportunity. Melanie obviously wasn't interested in being friends. Even Uncle Tobias and Aunt Georgina hadn't bothered to be home to greet her when she arrived.

Hattie placed the last of Constance's dresses in the oak wardrobe and turned to Constance with a smile.

"Don't you go being bothered by anything that Miss Melanie says," she told Constance. "She just needs to warm up to the idea of having another young lady as pretty as herself around the house. I've known Miss Melanie since she was a tiny baby. She's not really such a bad one, you'll see."

Constance bit her lip and looked away. She didn't want Hattie to see the tear rolling down her cheek.

A few moments later, Ezra came back into the room carrying the pitcher of water. "Here you are, Miss," he said.

"Thank you, Ezra," Hattie said reaching for the pitcher. "Now, run downstairs and see if Rachel needs help getting on the dinner. I'll reckon the Missus will be wanting fresh flowers for the table, too. She didn't have a chance to visit the gardens this morning."

With a smile for Constance, Ezra left the room, and Hattie turned back to Constance. "The Missus had to make a call on Mrs. Welles a few miles down. Mrs. Welles just had a new baby, and feels poorly."

"Oh," Constance said.

"Now step right out of that heavy dress so I can get it washed," Hattie went on. "We'll have you wear one of Miss Melanie's, until we can get your own made. That girl has more dresses than she can count."

Hattie helped Constance remove her dusty dress. As soon as the nursemaid left the room, Constance flopped down on the quilt in her petticoats and camisole. She felt more tired now than ever.

The next thing she knew, she was awakened by the sound of a bell being rung somewhere downstairs. Through the open window, Constance could hear distant church bells chiming noon.

Dinner! she realized with a start. Everyone would be waiting for her downstairs.

There was a knock on the door, and Hattie poked her head into the room. "Miss Constance, would you like a tray brought up?"

Constance almost said yes. She knew she had to meet her aunt and uncle sometime and she'd have to face Melanie again, sooner or later.

"No, thank you," Constance said. "I'll go down."

"All right, then," Hattie said. "Dinner will be served in the dining room. I've put a dress at the end of the bed for you."

A few minutes later, Constance had splashed cool water on her face, redone her braid, and slipped into one of Melanie's dresses, a pink one with a rose-colored sash.

Much better, Constance told her reflection in the mirror.

She left the cheerful bedroom and slowly descended the stairs, being careful not to look at the spooky portraits on the wall. When she reached the large double doors that led into the dining room, she saw that Toby, Melanie, and a distinguished-looking man and woman were already sitting at the long, shining table. *Uh-oh,* she thought, *late for my first meal.*

The man, who was well-dressed and had a red beard, rose immediately from his chair at the far end of the table. "Constance, I presume," he said. "I am your Uncle Tobias." His voice was low and serious.

The blonde woman at the other end of table smiled at Constance. Fair and elegant, she looked very much like Melanie. "And I'm your Aunt Georgina," she said. "We are so sorry we were not all here to greet you this morning. Please sit down," she added, as Constance hesitated in the doorway.

Constance stepped forward, and Toby rushed to pull out a chair for her next to Melanie. Constance could feel the other girl's eyes boring into her as she sat down. *She's probably going to say something about my wearing her dress,* Constance thought.

But Melanie turned away. "Father, where's Wood?"

"I am afraid he has been detained in Baltimore," Uncle Tobias said.

Melanie set her mouth in a pout as a bowl of steaming soup was set before her by one of the young women Constance had seen earlier. "He promised to take me for a drive this afternoon," she said.

"Don't you worry yourself about that," her father told her, his voice softening. "Wood is a gentleman of his word."

Just then, the double doors swung open, and a tall, dark-haired young man burst into the room.

"Wood!" Melanie said, her pout vanishing.

Aunt Georgina smiled. "You're just in time, Wood. Rachel, bring young Mr. Morgan his soup."

"Sit down, son," Uncle Tobias said. "We were just welcoming your cousin Constance. She arrived this morning."

The handsome young man nodded to Constance and took his place at the table. "I'm sorry I'm late, Mother. I've brought you all some very interesting news from Baltimore."

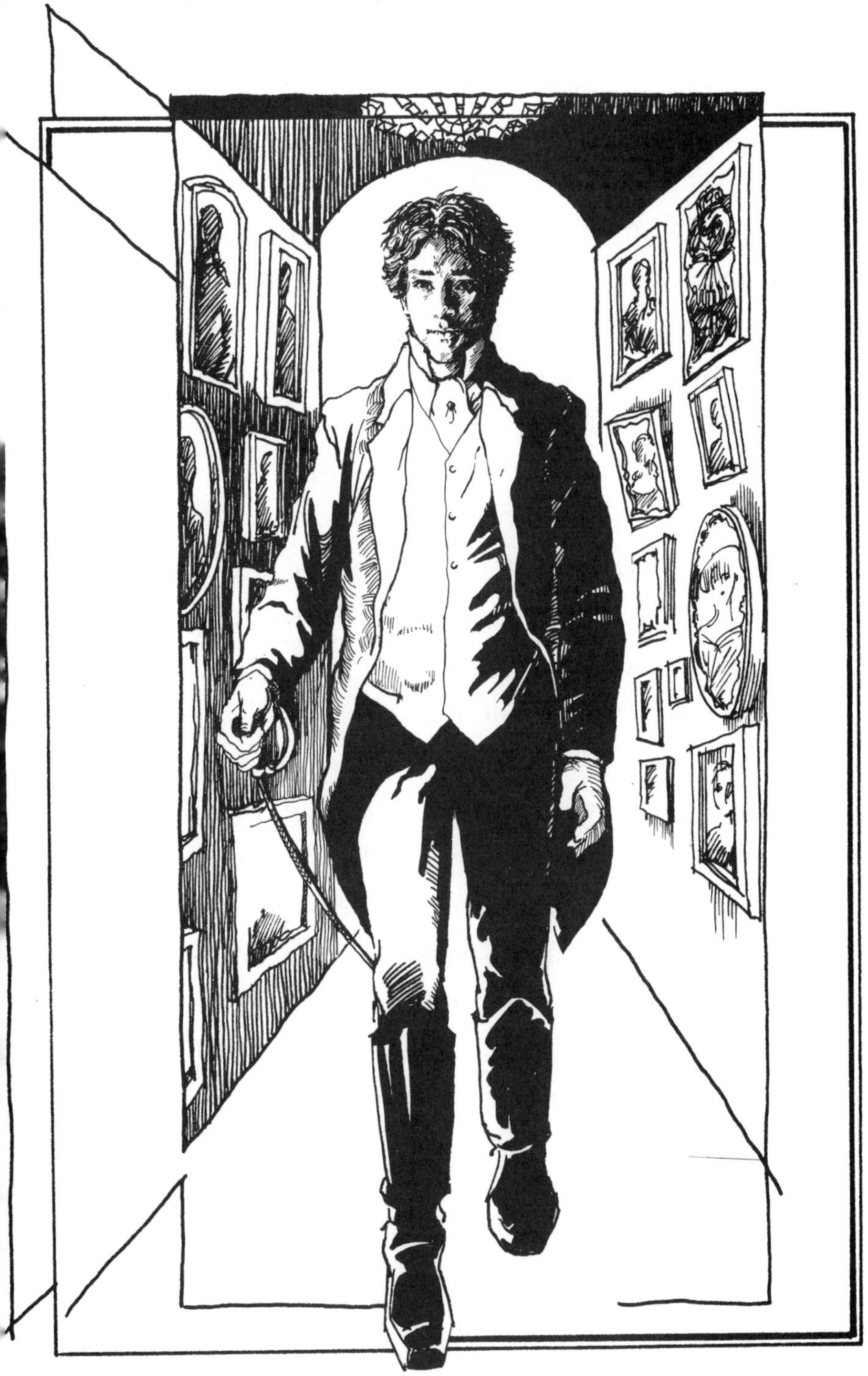

"What?" Toby said eagerly.

"Be quiet, Toby," Melanie said. Then she leaned forward across the table. "Do tell, Wood," she said, her eyes shining.

Constance gazed at her cousin in surprise. Melanie seemed ready to hang on her older brother's every word. *At least there's someone she listens to,* Constance thought.

Wood looked around the table. "President Lincoln has officially declared that an 'insurrection' exists," he said. "Today, he asked the governors of the Union states, including Maryland and Virginia, to supply seventy-five thousand volunteers. Those men who sign on will enlist for three months."

"This will mean war for sure," Uncle Tobias said grimly. "Virginia will secede immediately, and Governor Hicks will no doubt call the Maryland legislature together to vote on secession as well."

Constance sunk lower in her seat. Would the Morgans be angry now with people from the North? Even an eleven-year-old Yankee girl?

But no one seemed to notice her. Aunt Georgina's face was very pale. Toby dropped his soup spoon with a clatter. Even Melanie seemed speechless.

"And that's not all," Wood went on excitedly. "Jefferson Davis has called on the Confederate States' legislatures to provide one hundred thousand troops."

Uncle Tobias shook his head gravely. "I had hoped that war could be avoided," he said. "But now it appears that it is too late for peace."

"Well, I'm not going to wait for Maryland to secede from the Union," Wood said. "I'm planning to enlist in the Confederate Army right away."

Melanie clapped her hands. "Oh, Wood!" she cried. "You'll make such a brave, splendid soldier!"

Uncle Tobias stood up so quickly that he nearly knocked over his chair. "He will do no such thing!" he thundered, bringing his fist down on the table.

Wood stood up, too. "You can't stop me!" he said angrily.

"Oh!" Aunt Georgina cried breathlessly. Her face had gone even paler and she looked faint. Rachel who had been standing in the corner, rushed out of the room and reappeared with a bottle of smelling salts. She held it under Aunt Georgina's nose to revive her.

Uncle Tobias sat back down. "Son, you're too young to be a soldier," he said in a calmer voice.

"That's rubbish," Wood said. "There are lads of fifteen and sixteen already in line to enlist. I'll be eighteen next month. It is my duty to fight for the glory of the Confederacy."

"Your duty is to stay right here and help me run this plantation," Uncle Tobias said. "After all, it will be yours one day. Think of your poor mother, Wood."

Wood looked over at Aunt Georgina, who was starting to cry quietly. His handsome face flushed bright red and he looked down at the table for a moment. "Very well," he said finally. "I'll wait to enlist, for Mother's sake. But not for long," he added. With that, Wood turned on his heels and left the room.

No one said a word. Uncle Tobias's hand shook a bit as he motioned for Rachel to pour him more wine, and Aunt Georgina looked upset. Toby was fidgeting with his fork, and Constance did not dare glance sideways at Melanie. No one spoke for the rest of the meal. Constance gazed down at the honey-cured ham and sweet potatoes on her plate. She wasn't feeling hungry at all. It was a relief when the meal ended at last.

After dinner, Aunt Georgina retired upstairs, Uncle Tobias rode out to the tobacco fields, and Melanie went into the parlor to practice the piano.

"Cousin Constance, do you like to read?" Toby asked as the two of them stepped out into the hall.

"Oh, yes," Constance answered. "But Miss Finch didn't approve of young ladies reading books, except for the Bible. She said I should be spending more time at my needlework."

"My father has a fine library," Toby said. "He lets me read his books whenever I want. Would you like to see them?"

Constance nodded eagerly. She was glad that she and Toby had something in common. Maybe the two of them would be better friends than she and Melanie.

Toby led Constance to the east wing of the house. At the end of the hall, Constance could see a high-ceilinged room lined wall-to-wall with books.

Constance went straight to the wooden globe in

the center of the room. "It's beautiful," she said, giving the globe a spin.

"I'd like to be an explorer someday," Toby said, "or maybe a pirate."

Just then, Constance spotted Ezra curled in a large green armchair in the corner. He was looking at a big book of old maps. "Maybe Ezra wants to be an explorer, too," she said to Toby.

At the sound of Constance's voice, Ezra snapped shut the book and sprang out of the chair. "I — I just wanted to see the drawings of the sea monsters,"he said. "I didn't mean any harm."

"Don't go," Toby said. "Would you like me to show you some of the other things on those maps?"

Ezra's face lit up. "Yes, I would," he said. "I'm having trouble figuring out some of the names."

Constance followed Toby over to the armchair. Toby started to turn the pages, pointing out deserts, jungles, and rivers. Every now and then, Constance helped Ezra sound out a few of the harder words.

Suddenly, Melanie appeared in the doorway. "What are you doing?" she screeched.

"We're reading with Ezra," Constance said. This time she could not help frowning.

Melanie glared at her. "In case you didn't know, Cousin Constance, teaching a slave to read and write is against the law in the South. I'm going to tell my father!"

Constance stared at Melanie. She was so angry, she couldn't think of anything to say. Why was her cousin being so hateful? She looked over at Toby for help.

Her cousin just shrugged. "Don't mind Melanie," he said. "She's trying to scare you, that's all. It's not against the law to teach Ezra to read. Ezra belongs to our family. It's up to us."

Constance turned toward Ezra, who was looking down at the ground.

"It's not your fault," Constance said to him, clenching her jaw in anger. Suddenly, she couldn't stand being inside the house one more minute. She ran down the hall and out the nearest door.

Finding herself on the back lawn, Constance took a deep breath. The fresh air felt wonderful. She looked around the sprawling yard. Maybe she could find the gardens Hattie had mentioned earlier. Some new scenery might help her take her mind off horrible

Cousin Melanie.

She was just starting down the stone path when she spied a small, domed brick house not far behind the main house. Curious, she turned off onto another path and headed to the door of the little building.

To her surprise, it turned out to be a bustling, stiflingly hot kitchen. An open hearth stood at one end, and several chickens hung from hooks in the ceiling. Hattie was inside polishing silver. Several other women were cleaning pots and stacking platters.

"Miss Constance," Hattie said in surprise. "What are you doing here, child?"

"I'm just looking around," Constance said, watching a woman clean some carrots. Her eye caught a glint of gold on the wooden butcher block. It was a fancy watch on a chain. "What a pretty watch," she breathed. "May I see it?"

"Yes," Hattie said, nodding, "but only for a minute. I need to clean it right quick for the master." She picked up the watch and handed it to Constance.

"It's so beautiful," Constance said. "My father had one like it, I think." She turned the timepiece over in her hand. The initials "TRM" were engraved on the other side. Constance felt a sharp pang of loneliness. Her father had initials on his watch, too — JWM, for Joseph William Morgan.

She gave the watch back to Hattie and glanced around the kitchen. "I've never seen a kitchen outdoors before," she said.

"Well, this way, if there's a kitchen fire, the whole house won't burn down," Hattie said. "I've never seen a kitchen indoors, but I hear they have them in big towns."

Just then, a short, thin man with greased-back hair and a funny moustache appeared at the door. He was pushing a cart filled with pots and pans and pieces of tin. "Good afternoon," he said, tipping his hat. "Wilfred Wiley is the name."

"We don't want to buy anything," Hattie told him.

"Perhaps the mistress of the house would like to look at my collection of combs straight from Paris, France," the man said, rummaging through the cart.

"No, thank you," Hattie said firmly. "Good day."

Suddenly, the man leaned forward to look at the gold watch in Hattie's hands. "Well now, that's a mighty fine timepiece. Do you think your master would sell it?"

"Never," Hattie said, shaking her head.

"I'll give you twenty dollars for it," Mr. Wiley said.

Hattie put her hands on her hips. "Now see here, sir," she said. "I told you, this watch is not for sale."

"Why don't I speak to your master about it myself?" the tin man said. "Perhaps he might be persuaded..."

Hattie turned back to Constance. "Miss Constance, you run along now. The kitchen is no place for a young lady like yourself."

Constance nodded reluctantly and slowly left the

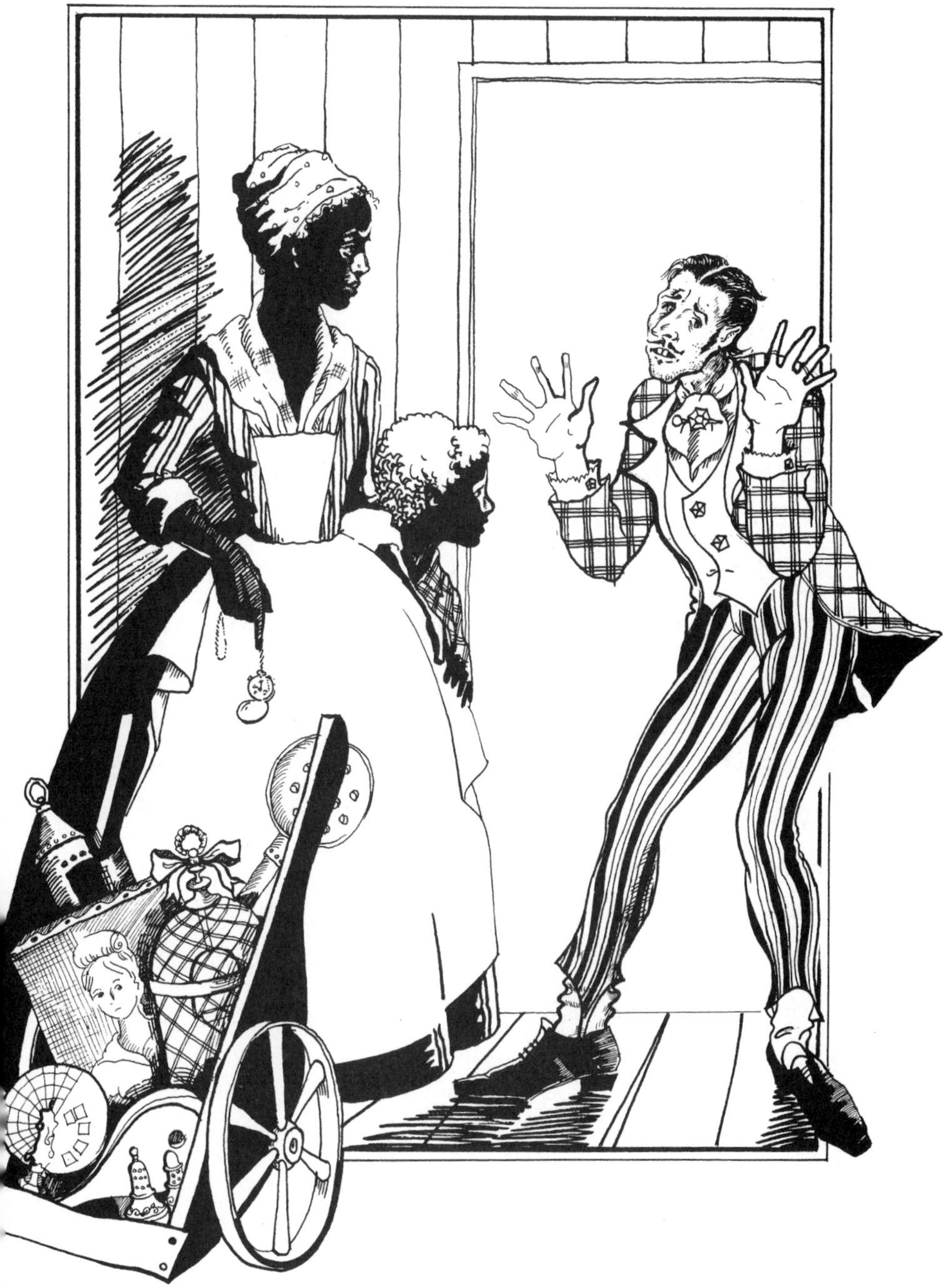

little brick building. She glanced back when she reached the main path, curious to see whether the tin salesman had finally left.

But Mr. Wiley was still arguing with Hattie about the watch. *He certainly isn't giving up*, Constance thought, shaking her head.

She continued down the path, still hoping to find the gardens. After she had walked for a few minutes without a glimpse of them, she decided to head back to the main house. The afternoon was very warm, and she was beginning to feel tired again.

Trudging up the hill, she caught sight of Mr. Wiley ahead of her. He was pushing his cart very fast toward the road and glancing over his shoulder.

He certainly looks worried, Constance thought. *Hattie must have sent him on his way in a hurry.*

As she drew nearer to the main house, Constance saw Melanie appear suddenly on the back porch. Her cousin was craning her neck, as though she were looking for someone. She seemed to be very upset.

When she spotted Constance, she began to wave her arms wildly. "Cousin Constance, come quickly!" she called.

Alarmed, Constance picked up her skirt and ran the rest of the way. "What is it?" she cried.

Melanie clasped her hands in front of her chest. "Something terrible has happened!" she said. "Father's gold watch has been stolen!"

5

"Can you believe this happened?" Melanie cried, wringing her hands. "Poor Father! That gold watch was his most prized possession. Grandfather gave it to him just before he died."

"Are you sure it's been stolen?" Constance asked. "Hattie was getting ready to polish it in the kitchen."

Melanie shook her head. "Hattie came up to the house to tell Mother the watch was missing. She said it was there on the butcher block one minute, and when she turned around to pick it up, it was gone. Father will be very upset when he finds out."

Constance immediately thought of Mr. Wiley, the strange man with the cart. Hadn't he wanted that watch very badly? And he'd left the grounds very quickly, looking back over his shoulder. Had he been worried that he was being followed?

Constance began to tell her cousin about Mr. Wiley. But Melanie was hardly listening.

"Hattie mentioned an unpleasant little man," she

said with a wave of her hand. "But I know exactly who stole Father's watch."

"Who?" Constance asked.

"Why, that little thief, Ezra." Melanie said.

"Ezra?" Constance said in surprise. "But why would he steal the watch from under his own mother's nose?"

Melanie rolled her eyes, as if Constance had asked a very silly question. "He's always poking around the house, getting into trouble. You saw what happened this morning. He took a book from my room."

"Maybe Ezra just likes to read," Constance said. "That doesn't mean he's a thief. Besides, Ezra wasn't in the kitchen. Only Hattie and some of the other women were there."

"You don't know what you're talking about," Melanie snapped. "Toby and Ezra both went looking for you after you ran out of the library like a silly goose. Of course Ezra could have taken the watch. I just know he did, and I'm going to get it back."

Melanie flounced back into the house. Constance hurried after her.

"Please wait, Melanie," she said. "If you'd seen that awful Mr. Wiley..."

"Hmmph," said Melanie.

Constance tried another approach. "Well, what would Ezra do with your father's watch? Maybe he just borrowed it to look at, like your book, and he's going to give it back."

"Not likely," Melanie said, as the two of them

passed the stairs. "He wouldn't dare let anyone know what he did, or he'd get a whipping for sure."

Constance stopped in her tracks and threw up her hands. "Toby went to the kitchen with Ezra. Wouldn't he have seen Ezra take the watch?"

Just then, Ezra appeared around the corner, looking frightened. "I didn't steal the watch, Miss Melanie," he said. "Honest, I didn't."

Melanie gave him a cool look. "We'll see about that."

Constance jumped as Toby suddenly stepped into the hall from behind the sitting room doors.

"What are you doing, sneaking around like that?" Melanie said angrily. "It's not polite to listen to other people's private conversations. Surely you're as bad as Ezra here."

Toby ignored his sister. "So who is this Mr. Wiley you were talking about, Cousin Constance?" he asked.

When Constance told him, he nodded gravely. "He sounds like a thief to me," he said.

"The real thief is right here," Melanie said, pointing at Ezra, who quickly turned away. "And I'm going to prove it!" She added and stormed off, her silk skirts rustling.

Ezra tore off in the other direction, and Toby turned to Constance. "We can't let Melanie go to Father with this," he said. "He'll believe her for sure. He always does. I know Ezra didn't do it. I've known him since he was a baby. He never lies."

"Well then," Constance said, tilting her chin.

"Why don't we find the real thief ourselves?"

Toby grinned. "Fine with me. Where shall we start?"

"That's easy," Constance told him. "We find Mr. Wiley. He was headed back on the road toward Baltimore, I think."

"Let's go, then," Toby said. "If we leave right away, maybe we can catch up with him."

"But how?" Constance said, frowning. "He's probably all the way to town by this time."

"Don't worry," Toby said. "I saw Wood's horse, tied up out front. We can hitch him to the cart."

"Do you think Wood will mind?" Constance asked, worried.

"Nah," Toby answered. "He's not around anywhere to ask. Besides, he can always take the carriage if he needs it."

A few minutes later, Constance was sitting next to Toby in a rickety wooden cart, as it jounced along the dirt road. "We'll have to watch very carefully for Mr. Wiley," she said.

Toby nodded. "You look to the right," he said. "I'll look to the left. Maybe he's making other stops along the way to town."

Constance coughed and covered her face with her hands as the cart kicked up dust along the road. "I can hardly see anything," she said. "But we'll have to try."

Toby urged the horse to quicken his pace. "You know," he said after a moment, "I felt right sorry for you at dinner today, having to listen to Wood and Father arguing like that. Especially it being your first day with us and all. But Wood and Father never seem to see eye to eye. Father thinks Maryland should stay in the Union. Wood thinks Maryland should secede, as soon as possible. The only thing they agree on is that Father should keep his slaves. Wood thinks it's a white man's right. Father may give our slaves their freedom someday, but not for a long time. He says he needs slave labor to keep the plantation running."

"I've never known any slaves," Constance said. "But I don't think it's right that people should be owned by other people."

Toby didn't answer right away. Then he said, "I believe in states' rights and I love the South," he said. "But I'm still not sure whether Maryland should secede or not. The only thing I'm sure of is that slavery is wrong. I'd like to see Father free every one of his slaves. And I think Mother feels the same way."

"I suppose Melanie doesn't think much of that notion," Constance said, thinking of the superior way her cousin treated Ezra.

Toby snorted. "Melanie thinks whatever Wood does."

Constance thought Toby sounded a little jealous. But she couldn't really blame him. Melanie did seem to prefer her older brother. Wood was her idol.

"It wouldn't even surprise me," Toby went on, "if Melanie took Father's watch herself, just so she could say Ezra stole it. She loves to see Ezra get in trouble."

"But why?" Constance asked.

"I'm not sure," Toby said, with a shrug. "Sometimes I get the feeling she misses having Hattie's full attention. When Hattie and her husband John, one of the field hands, had Ezra, Hattie stopped paying as much attention to Melanie and me. Ezra takes up a lot of Hattie's time. Anyway, Ezra's young and he's a slave, so he can't stand up to Melanie."

"Oh," Constance said, trying to sort all of this out.

Just then, she noticed that the buildings had grown very close together, and that the road was growing more and more crowded. It was getting noisier, too, with shouting people and pounding horse hooves and crying children.

"We'd best leave the cart outside those shops over there," Toby said. "We'll have a better chance of spotting your tin man on foot."

"He's short and thin," Constance said. "With very black, shiny hair, all combed back. He has a moustache, too."

Toby hitched the horse and cart to a post and helped Constance down. Then he took the wooden bucket from beside the post and filled it with water from a nearby well.

Suddenly, it seemed as if people were pushing closer and closer to her, and she lost sight of Toby.

"I think I see him!" she heard Toby say from somewhere to her left. "Wait here, and I'll try to catch him."

Constance felt relieved that they had found the tin man so quickly. What would Toby say to him? Would he have the watch? She found herself beginning to worry as the crowd grew larger.

Where is Toby? she thought. *Why didn't he wait for me, and what are all these people doing?*

Then she realized that someone was giving a speech on top of a platform a few feet away. She couldn't see him well, but she could hear him declaring that Maryland should secede from the Union.

"Never!" a man called from the crowd.

"The North has more men," another person shouted. "And more factories and foundries and shipyards. They have better railroads and steamboat lines, too."

"Gentlemen," the man on the platform shouted to the crowd, "What about states' rights? What about slavery? Remember the great cause for which we will fight to the death: the Confederacy!"

"We can teach those Yankee boys a lesson!" someone behind Constance called.

A great shout came up from the crowd. Constance began to panic as the crowd grew larger and more tightly packed together.

I can't breathe! she thought. *I'll be squeezed to death.*

The crowd became noisier by the minute, and Constance felt herself endlessly shoved and jostled.

Suddenly, she was pushed backward and lost her balance. With a helpless cry, she fell beneath a sea of feet.

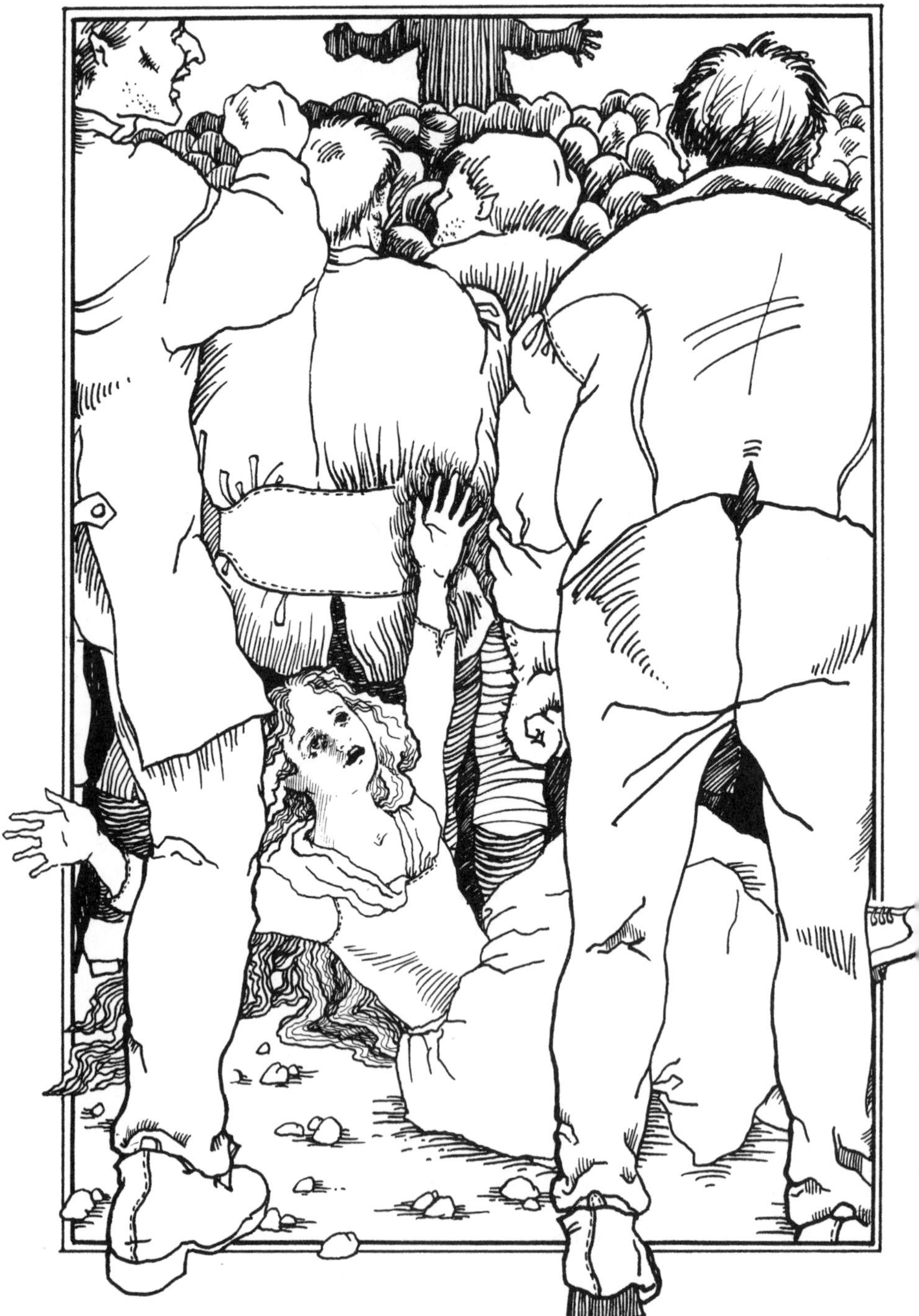

Constance gasped for air as the crowd closed in. A boot dug into her side, and she cried out as someone stepped on her hand.

Suddenly, two strong arms reached down and grabbed her under the arms. "Are you all right, Cousin Constance?" a deep voice said.

Constance twisted around. Wood was frowning down at her.

"I'm taking you out of here," he said grimly. "This is no place for a young girl." Before she knew it, Constance was being half-pulled, half-carried through the crowd by her older cousin. "Make way!" Wood called above the din. "We have a child here!"

Constance winced at being called a child. But she knew Wood was only trying to help. She breathed a sigh of relief as the crowd began to part for them.

"I have a horse hitched to that tree over there," Wood said as they reached the edge of the crowd. "I'm going to take you straight home."

Constance didn't know what to say. She wasn't sure where Toby was, and she wanted to stay and hunt for Mr. Wiley. But she knew she should be grateful that Wood had rescued her. So she simply nodded and said, "Thank you for helping me back there."

Wood gave a short laugh. "My pleasure," he said. "I'd say you were in a fair piece of trouble, being trampled by all those boots. What in blazes were you doing at a Confederate rally?"

Constance decided not to tell her older cousin that she had been hunting for a thief. Maybe he didn't know yet about his father's missing watch. And she certainly didn't want him going after Ezra when they got back to the plantation. "I came with Toby," she said finally. "He was just showing me the city."

Wood's dark brows furrowed his handsome face. "I can't say that was wise on my brother's part," he said. "He should have known better than to have dragged you here."

"Oh, no," Constance said quickly. "I wanted to see Baltimore — truly I did."

"Well, now you've seen it," Wood said. "Where is Toby, anyway?"

Constance felt her face grow warm. She wasn't used to telling lies. "I-I'm not sure," she answered. "He said he'd be back shortly."

Wood mumbled something under his breath about Toby catching blazes when he got home.

Pain shot through her side as Wood lifted her into

the saddle of a tall chestnut-colored horse. Her whole body felt sore and she wasn't looking forward to the ride home. Constance always felt uneasy around horses.

Wood seemed to detect her nervousness. "Never been on a horse before, eh?"

"Only a few times," Constance admitted.

"Well, don't fret, cousin," Wood said, chuckling. "I'll hold onto you so you don't fall. I reckon young ladies don't ride much in the middle of Philadelphia. My sister prefers the carriage herself."

After Wood had mounted the horse and settled behind her in the saddle, they started out of town.

Constance sneaked a peek at her older cousin. *Wood was nice enough,* she thought, *but he seemed to have other things on his mind.* She had a feeling he was annoyed about not being able to stay at the rally but was trying not to show it.

As they passed a row of dingy-looking shops, a glint of gold in one of the windows caught Constance's eye. She barely contained her gasp. It was a handsome watch hanging on a fancy gold chain! Arranged around the watch was an odd assortment of items, including a battered-looking hat, an ugly fringed lamp, a set of boot brushes, bundled stacks of piano music, and a tarnished teapot. None of them seemed new.

Could that be Uncle Tobias's watch? Constance thought excitedly. She leaned over the edge of the saddle, trying to catch a closer glimpse of the timepiece.

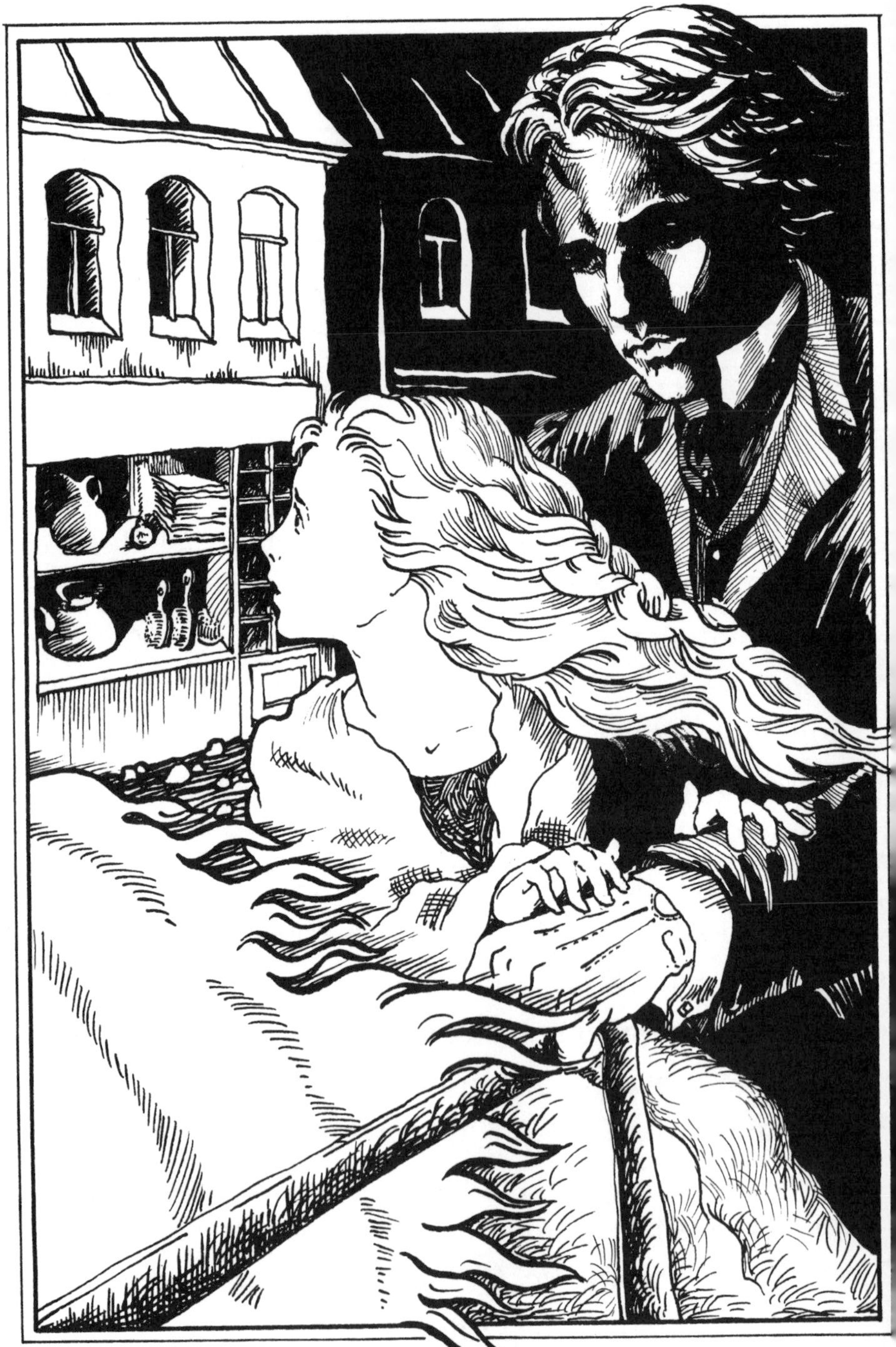

"Easy there, Cousin Constance," Wood said, his hand tightening on her waist.

"I was trying to see a — a lovely teapot in that shop window," Constance said. "May we turn back and see it?"

Wood shook his head. "I think you've seen enough for one day. Besides, Mother would be very upset if I didn't bring you straight home. She was right worried when she found out you and Toby were gone, especially with a strange man on the grounds and all."

So Wood does know about Mr. Wiley, Constance thought. *And the stolen watch, too, most likely.* "Has the thief been found?" she asked aloud.

"No," Wood said. "But my sister thinks Ezra took Father's watch. I'm inclined to believe her, but Mother keeps saying we can't be sure."

Once again, Constance decided not to bring up Mr. Wiley. Her cousin would probably be angry to hear that she and Toby had been chasing a strange man all by themselves.

She wondered whether Toby had found the tin man. Would Mr. Wiley try to hurt Toby if Toby accused him of being a thief? He didn't look dangerous, but one could never tell.

No, Constance reassured herself. *There were too many people around for Mr. Wiley to go after Toby.* She hoped Toby wouldn't do anything rash. She wished the two of them had figured out the last part of their plan to get Uncle Tobias's watch back.

When Wood and Constance arrived at the plantation, Aunt Georgina was waiting for them on the front porch.

"Constance!" she cried as Constance and Wood rode up. "Thank heavens you've been found. Where is Toby?"

"He's still in town, I'm afraid," Wood told his mother as he helped Constance from the horse. "I'm heading straight back to get him." With a nod, he turned his horse around and galloped toward the road again.

Aunt Georgina began to fuss over Constance. "You gave us all such a fright, my dear," she said. "Whatever possessed you and Toby to run off like that?"

Just then, Hattie appeared on the porch. "Don't fret, Ma'am," she told Constance's aunt. "I'll take Miss Constance straight to her room and get her cleaned up. Then she can take a nice, long rest."

"Thank you, Hattie," Aunt Georgina said. "That's a fine idea."

Constance shook her head. She really didn't want to take a rest. "Oh, no —" she began, but Hattie had already started to lead her away. "Now you just hush yourself, Miss Constance," she said. "You need to get your strength back."

Even though Constance told herself she wasn't tired anymore, she had to admit that the warm sponge bath Hattie gave her did make her sore legs feel a lot better.

Then Hattie helped her get into a starched white nightgown. "Now where did you get all them black and blue marks?" she asked, frowning as she tucked Constance into bed. "And that nasty scratch on your arm? What were you foolish children doing in the town?"

Before Constance could answer, there was a knock at the door.

"Come in," Constance called.

The door opened, and Toby stepped into the room. Constance smiled, glad to see that her cousin was all right.

"I'm sorry about what happened, Cousin Constance," Toby said, hanging his head. "I didn't mean to run off and leave you like that. I had no idea you might get hurt."

Constance had to feel sorry for him. After all, she was the one who'd wanted to find the tin man in the first place.

Toby looked up again and grinned sheepishly. "Wood ran into me on the road," he said. "He dragged me out of the cart and gave me the dickens. I'm really going to catch it when Father gets back from the fields."

Hattie put her hands on her hips. "Now see here," she said. "I want to know exactly what happened to you children. Why did you ever get it into your foolish heads to go into town by yourselves?"

Constance and Toby exchanged glances.

Constance decided it was time to tell someone the truth. Toby gave her a nod.

"We wanted to find Mr. Wiley," Constance said. "You know, that awful tin man who wanted to buy Uncle Tobias's watch. We're sure he stole it, and —"

"Miss Constance," Hattie broke in gently. "That was right nice of you and Master Toby. But Mr. Wiley didn't take that watch."

"He didn't?" Constance and Toby said together.

Hattie shook her head. "No, indeed," she said. "I sent that pesky gentleman off faster than a greased hog. And I watched out to make sure he didn't come back. The master's watch was still in my hands when he left."

"Oh," Constance said, disappointed. Toby looked troubled, too.

Hattie sighed. "I just can't figure this out," she said. "Ezra was in the kitchen for a minute, all right. But I know he'd never steal the master's fine watch. He's been looking for it all afternoon."

"I don't think Ezra took the watch, either," Constance said.

The nursemaid shook her head. "It don't make sense, Miss Constance. The only people in that kitchen was me and the girls. Then there was you, Master Toby, Ezra, and Miss Melanie."

Constance froze. *Aha!* she thought. *Melanie!*

7

As soon as Hattie and Toby left the room, Constance threw back the quilt and jumped out of bed. Her mind was buzzing with excitement.

Maybe Toby was right, she thought. Maybe Melanie did steal Uncle Tobias's watch herself, just to get Ezra in trouble. She certainly seemed to dislike Hattie's son. And Melanie was so spoiled and mean that Constance wouldn't be surprised if her cousin had planned the whole thing to get more attention for herself.

Constance went over to the wardrobe and took out one of her heavy black dresses. She pulled it quickly over her head and reached under the bed for her shoes. Then she hurried to the doorway and peered up and down the hall. No one was there.

This is my chance, Constance thought.

With her heart pounding, she made her way down the hall to Melanie's room. She hesitated outside the door, unable to bring herself to knock.

What if Melanie was inside? She didn't want to

talk to her cousin yet. Not until she knew for sure that Melanie was the thief. And the only way she could find out the truth was to catch Melanie red-handed with Uncle Tobias's watch.

Constance took a deep breath and rapped on Melanie's door.

There was no answer.

Sighing with relief, Constance crept inside the room. It was much fancier than her own, with expensive drapes, a huge mahogany wardrobe, a blue velvet chair, and an elaborate canopy bed. Although the room was right next door to Constance's, it seemed dark and gloomy by comparison. Then Constance realized that Melanie kept the curtains drawn.

She walked over to the dressing table on the other side of the room. Brushes and combs and hairpins were neatly laid out on the lace-covered tabletop. Constance picked up a framed silver picture of the Morgans and peered at it closely.

Suddenly, Constance heard light footsteps coming down the hall. She hastily put down the picture, nearly knocking over a small bottle of perfume, and hurried behind the large blue velvet chair.

The door opened, and Melanie walked in. She went directly to the dressing table and leaned toward her reflection in the mirror. She adjusted a loose blonde curl and pinched her cheeks to make them redder.

Toby was right, Constance thought, peeking around the chair. Cousin Melanie certainly does a good deal of primping.

Then Melanie reached toward a small brown box on the dressing table. Constance had been so busy looking at the picture that she hadn't even noticed it. She watched Melanie's reflection in the mirror as her cousin took a small key from the pocket of her dress and started to open the box.

Constance stifled a gasp. *Was Uncle Tobias's watch inside that box?* she wondered.

There was a knock at the door and Melanie snapped the box shut and quickly turned around, stuffing the key inside her pocket again. "Yes?" she called.

Constance crouched lower behind the chair again, as Hattie poked her head inside the door.

"Excuse me, Miss Melanie," the nursemaid said. "I'm looking for your Cousin Constance. When I left her, she was fixin' to take a nap. Now she's up and disappeared on me again."

Oh, no! Constance thought. *What will Hattie and Melanie say if they find me here? They'll think I stole Uncle Tobias's watch if they catch me sneaking around someone else's room.*

Melanie sniffed. "Well, I haven't seen her," she said. "If you ask me, that Yankee girl is a peck of trouble. She's probably run off with Toby again."

"All right, Miss Melanie. Supper's at six o'clock." Hattie closed the door, and Constance peered around the chair.

Melanie was opening the box. Constance held her

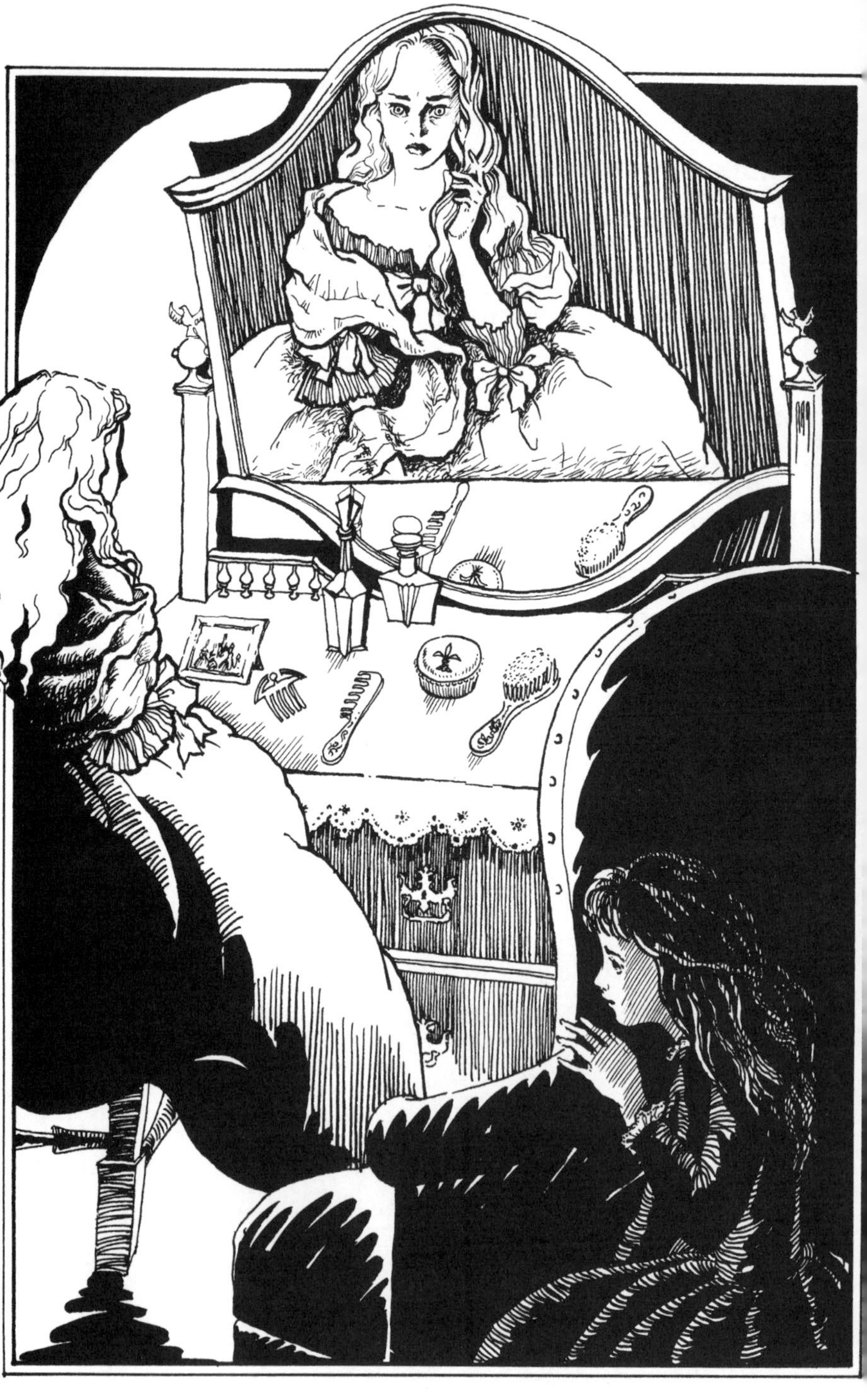

breath as her cousin brought out a pair of pearl ear-bobs and put them on. She reached in again and took out a green velvet ribbon.

There can't be much else in that little box, Constance thought, feeling disappointed. *Melanie's just locking up her own jewelry. Did that mean Melanie herself was worried about the thief?*

She waited as Melanie tied the ribbon in her hair and sprayed herself lightly with perfume. Finally, her cousin left the room.

As soon as she was sure Melanie had disappeared down the hall, Constance hurried back to her own bedroom. It was only a matter of time before the whole household started looking for her. She kicked off her shoes and climbed back into the bed again, pulling the covers up to her chin.

A few minutes later, she heard Hattie's voice floating down the hall. "I'm telling you, Mrs. Morgan, that child is nowhere to be found," Hattie was saying. "I wasn't gone but a minute and she was out of that bed."

The door opened, and Aunt Georgina walked in. Hattie was right behind her.

Constance squeezed her eyes shut tightly.

"I'm afraid you're mistaken, Hattie," Aunt Georgina said. "Why, Constance is fast asleep. The poor little dear, she's had such a trying day. We won't disturb her for supper."

When Constance heard the door close, she opened her eyes, thinking about the stolen watch.

Could she be wrong about Ezra? After all, she didn't know the boy very well. But she kept hearing him pleading with Melanie. *I didn't steal the watch. Honest, I didn't.* He'd sounded so upset and no one had any proof that Ezra did steal the watch.

But I have no proof Melanie took it, Constance reminded herself. As far as she knew, neither Ezra nor Melanie had left the plantation all day. And there was still the question of the gold watch she'd seen in the shop window that afternoon. If the watch was indeed her uncle's, then Mr. Wiley had to be the thief. He must have stolen the watch and sold it that afternoon in Baltimore. *But how am I going to get a closer look at that watch?* Constance wondered. It was almost night-fall, and Uncle Tobias was probably home by now.

I have to talk to him, Constance told herself, before Melanie tells him that Ezra stole the watch. She threw back the covers and jumped out of bed again.

It was too late. When Constance arrived down-stairs a few minutes later, breathless, the Morgans were already gathered at the supper table.

"Good evening, Constance," Uncle Tobias said, nodding when she walked into the dining room.

Both Wood and Toby rushed to pull out her chair.

"How are you feeling now, my dear?" Aunt Georgina asked.

"I do believe she's late for another meal," Melanie said, unfolding her napkin.

"Hush, Melanie," her mother said sharply.

"We have been discussing the disturbing matter of my missing watch," Uncle Tobias told Constance. "And the way in which it might have disappeared."

"Father, I'm telling you, Ezra took it," Melanie said.

"And I'm sure it was that Mr. Wiley," Toby said hotly. "Or maybe it was YOU!"

"Me?" Melanie said, shocked. "Why, you—!"

"Children, please," Aunt Georgina broke in. "All of this ridiculous talk will upset your digestion."

Everyone fell silent as Ezra and another young slave entered the dining room. Ezra carried a basket of orange rolls, and the other boy held a tray of sliced vegetables.

Constance smiled at Ezra as he placed a roll on her plate, but he didn't smile back. She saw that his hand was shaking as he moved to Melanie's place. Her cousin was watching him intently.

Constance frowned. *That girl has a rude habit of staring at people,* she thought. *Especially people she doesn't like.*

Suddenly, Melanie reached out and grabbed Ezra by the collar. Startled, he dropped the basket, and a dozen sticky orange rolls tumbled to the floor.

"Look at this!" Melanie cried, still tugging at Ezra's shirt. "You all wanted proof that he's a thief. Well, now you have it! Ezra stole Father's watch and sold it!"

As Melanie shook Ezra, Constance and the rest of the Morgans watched in horror as a handful of green bills fluttered out of the little boy's shirt.

8

Constance sat paralyzed in her chair. Had she been wrong about Ezra after all?

Uncle Tobias rose to his feet. "Ezra, what is the meaning of this?" he said. "Where did you get that money?"

"I — I don't know, sir," Ezra stammered, backing away from the table.

"Well, I know," Melanie said. "You sold Father's watch."

Ezra shook his head. "I didn't touch Master Morgan's watch," he insisted. "I swear it on the Bible."

"Come now, young Ezra," Wood said sternly, as Toby jumped up and began to gather the bills from the floor. "How do you explain all that money stuffed inside your shirt?"

Just then, Hattie hurried into the dining room. "Oh, Mr. Morgan, Mrs. Morgan," she said, wringing her hands. "Rachel told me what happened. My Ezra is a good boy. He'd never lay a hand on nothing that wasn't his."

Aunt Georgina leaned across the table. "I'm sure Hattie is right, Tobias," she said. "There must be some other explanation."

"Well, I'd surely like to hear it," said Wood, leaning back in his chair and folding his arms.

"I can't imagine a scrap of a boy like Ezra selling a fancy watch in town," Aunt Georgina said. "And him a slave, as well. Whoever would buy a valuable item like that from the child without asking his master?"

Mr. Wiley, no doubt, Constance answered silently, but she kept quiet. She didn't want to make the case against Ezra seem any stronger. At least Aunt Georgina seemed to be taking his side.

She looked over at Toby, who had returned to his seat. Her cousin was staring down at his plate. *He feels as bad as I do,* Constance thought.

"I truly hope I'm wrong about this," Melanie began, "but another slave could have sold the watch for Ezra. Why, even Hattie?"

"Melanie!" the nursemaid cried in horror.

Aunt Georgina frowned at her daughter. "Hattie was right here on the plantation all day."

"That's enough, all of you," Uncle Tobias broke in. "Hattie, take Ezra into the pantry while I decide what to do."

Constance watched as Hattie led Ezra from the room.

"This is a most disturbing matter," Uncle Tobias said. "As you know, I am quite fond of Hattie and Ezra. But there is no denying that the boy was in possession of money that did not belong to him. And I will not tolerate thievery in this house."

"I reckon a whipping would knock a bit of sense into the boy, " Wood said.

Constance shuddered. *A whipping!* Wood didn't even seem willing to give Ezra a chance.

Uncle Tobias shook his head. "No," he said. "That will not be necessary. I will sell Hattie and Ezra off the plantation."

"No, Father!" Toby cried. "If you do that, Hattie and Ezra might be sold into hard labor!"

Aunt Georgina put a hand on Toby's arm. "Hush, Toby," she said. Then she turned to her husband. "Tobias, it would be shameful to split up Hattie and John's family like that."

"They're slaves, Mother," Wood said. "They belong to Father, and he can do whatever he likes with them."

That's not fair! Constance wanted to shout, but she didn't dare. If Wood and Uncle Tobias became angry with her, they might turn her out of the house. Then where would she go?

Poor Ezra and Hattie, Constance thought. Her eyes filled with tears, and she looked over at Melanie.

"Father." Melanie spoke up. To Constance's surprise, her voice seemed to tremble. "Please don't send Hattie away. She's been my nursemaid forever and ever, and Toby's and Wood's, too. We'd all miss her terribly, and I — I'm afraid I haven't been very fair to Ezra." She looked toward the pantry. "What if I was wrong about him being the thief?"

Constance stared at her cousin, shocked. Was hateful Melanie actually having a change of heart?

Uncle Tobias held up his hand. "I'm sorry, my dear, but I've made up my mind," he said. "There is a small chance that Ezra is innocent. But if so, then selling him and his mother will serve as a lesson to the other slaves — perhaps even to the real thief."

Constance's heart dropped straight to her shoes.

Uncle Tobias looked around the table. "However," he went on, "I will ask no questions if the watch is returned to me by tomorrow evening. Then Hattie and Ezra may stay. Is that understood?"

Constance's eyes met Toby's. *We have to find that watch*, she told him silently. Toby looked miserable, his freckled face pale and drawn.

When the children were excused from the table after the meal, Constance waited for Toby outside the dining room. But to her dismay, he ran past her like a shot. She started to follow him, but Melanie stepped into her path. "Is Wood coming out?" she asked, craning her neck to see through the doorway. "I must speak to him." Constance didn't answer. She was in too much of a hurry.

She ran down the hall after Toby, but he was

nowhere in sight. Where did he go? she wondered.

Suddenly, someone grasped her by the arm. It was Rachel. "Come along, Miss Constance," the young woman said.

"I promised Hattie I wouldn't let you run off again tonight," Rachel said, dragging Constance toward the stairs.

Constance started to protest, but Rachel's arm was firm. "Don't give me any nonsense," she warned. "Or both you and I will be in a heap of trouble."

Constance bit her lip in frustration as Rachel practically pulled her up the stairs. She didn't want to go to her room. Maybe after everyone had retired for the night, she could sneak around the house and look for Uncle Tobias's watch again.

To Constance's dismay, she soon discovered that plan wasn't going to work tonight. Rachel locked the door behind her after she had helped Constance get ready for bed. She even took the candle.

With a sigh, she crawled into bed. *I'll just have to get an early start in the morning,* she told herself. And she knew exactly where she was heading: straight back to Baltimore. She had to find that shop where she'd seen the fancy gold watch.

The next morning, Constance's breakfast was brought to her room on a tray. "Good morning, Miss Constance," Rachel said.

Constance eyed the eggs, ham, and biscuits on

her plate. She wasn't hungry at all. She was too anxious to speak to Toby. Surely he would go with her to the city again. They'd both be in serious trouble if anyone discovered they were missing from the plantation, but they had to find that watch.

Constance gulped down her breakfast and hurried downstairs, but Toby was nowhere to be found. "He said something about going fishing," Melanie told Constance sounding glum. She was sitting at the piano, staring at the keys with her hands clasped in her lap.

Constance wondered if Melanie was still upset about last night. Or maybe she was just feeling lonely and out of sorts. Constance didn't have time to talk to her cousin right now, and she couldn't waste precious minutes looking for Toby, either. Why on earth would he have gone fishing? She would just have to make her way into Baltimore on her own. But how?

Constance gazed out the sitting room window and spotted Peter, one of the stable boys, hitching up a chestnut mare to the cart she and Toby had taken into town the day before. The cart was filled with boxes and jugs.

She rushed outside and up to Peter, who was just climbing into the front of the cart. "Are you heading into town?" she asked him breathlessly.

"Yes, Miss," he said. "I'm on my way to market. Do you want to ride along?"

"Please," Constance replied, jumping into the cart next to him. What a stroke of luck! She quickly glanced over her shoulder to see whether Melanie was looking out the window, but she saw no sign of her cousin — or anyone else, either. Soon the cart was rattling along the bumpy road to town.

Constance began to grow anxious as they entered the city. How would she ever find the shop again? She thought she recognized the tree where Wood had hitched his horse, and the bunting-draped platform where the speeches had been given was still standing. Then she saw a row of familiar-looking shops. Another stroke of luck! Constance thought, feeling relieved. This had all been so much easier than she'd expected.

"You're not getting out, are you, Miss?" Peter asked in surprise, as Constance jumped down from the cart. "I can't just leave you here."

Constance gazed over his shoulder at a large building that stood not far from the bustling market-place. "What is that over there?" she asked, pointing.

He shaded his eyes. "That's the depot, Miss," he said. "There should be a train arriving soon."

"I'll meet you in front of the depot in half an hour," Constance told him, stepping back from the cart. "It should be easy enough to spot me there."

"Yes, Miss," he said. He sounded doubtful, but he drove the cart off toward the marketplace.

A few minutes later, Constance stood staring into the window of the very same shop she had noticed the day before. Sure enough, the gold watch was still there, looking more beautiful than ever.

Constance held her small black purse close to her chest. She had quite a few dollars left from the money Miss Finch had given her. If it wasn't enough to buy the watch, perhaps the shopkeeper would take what she had now and put the watch aside. That way, she could tell Uncle Tobias the whole story and come back later to pay the rest.

The bell above the door jingled as Constance walked in.

The shopkeeper, a very tall bearded man who looked a bit like her uncle, looked up. "May I help you, young lady?"

"Yes, please," Constance said, trying to sound grown up. "I'd like to see the watch in the window."

The shopkeeper nodded and walked over to get the watch. "This is a very fine piece," he said, handing it to her.

Her heart pounding, Constance turned the watch over in her hand. Sure enough, the initials engraved in fancy script on the back read TRM. It was Uncle Tobias's watch!

"It's worth at least one hundred dollars," the shopkeeper said. "But I'll part with it for seventy-five."

Seventy-five dollars! Constance thought, gulping. She didn't have anywhere near that much money. "This watch belongs to my uncle," she told the shopkeeper. "Did a short, thin man with a funny moustache bring it in to sell?"

"No," the shopkeeper said, frowning.

"Was the person a slave of about eight years?"

"Certainly not," the shopkeeper said indignantly. "I don't buy from slaves."

So it wasn't Ezra or another one of Uncle Tobias's slaves, Constance told herself. *But it wasn't Mr. Wiley, either.*

She took a deep breath. "Was it a girl around my age with blonde hair?"

"I beg your pardon, Miss!" the shopkeeper said. He sounded very angry now. "I don't keep track of every single person who comes through these doors with something to sell. As it happens, I do remember the fine young lad who sold me this watch. I am quite sure that it does not belong to your uncle." He reached out and snatched the timepiece from Constance's hand.

A fine young lad? Constance wondered. Could that have been Wood? Or —

Her mouth dropped open in horror. Suddenly, she had a feeling she knew who had taken Uncle Tobias's watch. And she needed to find that person right away.

Whirling around, Constance rushed out the door of the shop — and straight into Toby Morgan!

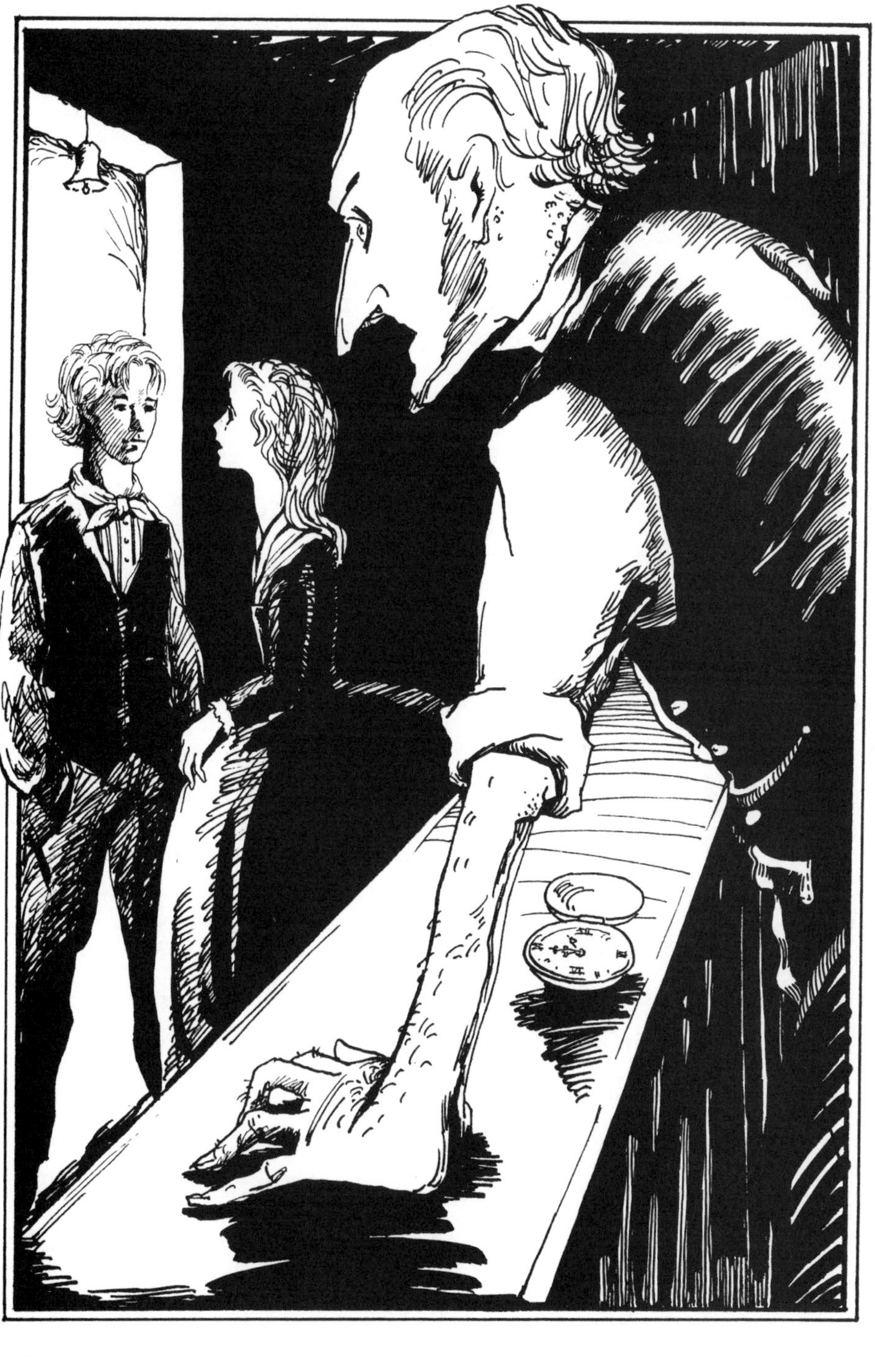

9

Constance stepped back and folded her arms. "Why, Cousin Toby," she said, frowning. "What are you doing here?"

"I was about to ask you the same thing," Toby said.

"I was looking for your father's watch," Constance said.

"Me, too," Toby said.

"But you already knew it was in this shop, didn't you?" Constance asked. She took a deep breath, waiting for her cousin's response. If her hunch was wrong, Toby would probably never be her friend again. And if it was right, she didn't know what she was going to do.

"What do you mean?" Toby said, but Constance saw him flush.

"You took the watch and sold it to that shopkeeper back there."

"That isn't true," Toby said hotly. "I — I was just coming into the shop to take a look around."

"You, Ezra, and Melanie were in the cookhouse when the watch disappeared," Constance said.

"So was Mr. Wiley," Toby pointed out. He looked around anxiously. "By the way, have you seen that no-good rascal around anywhere?"

"The shopkeeper just told me that a red-haired boy sold him that watch in the window," Constance went on. "That leaves you, Toby Morgan."

Toby didn't answer. He scowled and kicked at a pebble on the walk.

"And when your father said he'd sell Hattie and Ezra, you decided to try to get the watch back," Constance went on. "Isn't that so? But why did you even take it in the first place?"

Toby still didn't reply. He moved aside as a well-dressed man wearing a long coat and a top hat stepped from the street to gaze into the shop window.

"My, what a handsome watch," Constance heard the man murmur. "I must take a closer look." The bell over the shop door jingled as he walked inside.

Constance and Toby gazed at each other in horror. "Well, this is a fine mess," Constance said angrily. "What if that man buys your father's watch?"

"We won't let him do that," Toby said. "Don't worry, I'll handle this." He followed the man into the shop.

"Wait!" Constance called, hurrying after her cousin. But Toby was already inside, pretending to look at a display of glass jars holding different kinds of hard and soft candies. The well-dressed gentleman was just approaching the shopkeeper behind the counter.

"What are you going to do?" Constance whispered, coming up beside Toby.

Her cousin pulled a wad of bills tied with string from his pocket. "I'm going to buy the watch back," he said. "I have all the shopkeeper gave me for it."

"So you did steal the watch!" Constance said, furious. "And poor Ezra almost —"

"Shh!" Toby said. "It isn't the way it looks. I'll explain everything to you as soon as we get the watch back."

"Well, I should hope so," Constance muttered. She gazed back at the counter over a jar of caramels. The shopkeeper had brought the watch out from the window and was handing it to the other customer.

"A fine watch," the gentleman said, inspecting it closely. "Very fine indeed."

"You have excellent taste," the shopkeeper said approvingly. "And that piece keeps very good time, I might add."

The gentleman nodded. "How much do you want for it?"

The shopkeeper stroked his chin thoughtfully. "It's worth at least three hundred dollars," he said. "But for a fine gentleman like yourself, the price is two hundred and fifty dollars."

Constance gasped, quickly clapping a hand over

her mouth when the two men turned in her direction. "He told me seventy-five," she whispered to Toby, after the men had gone back to their conversation.

Toby sighed. "I guess we're out of luck. That weasel of a shopkeeper only gave me fifty for it."

Constance's eyes widened in disbelief. "You mean, you don't have enough money to buy the watch back?"

Toby shook his head glumly.

Constance bit back tears. She had fifty dollars in her purse. With Toby's fifty, they'd have only a hundred dollars between them.

"That sounds like a fair price for such a handsome watch," the man in the top hat said. Constance's heart beat faster as he began to count out bills into the shopkeeper's hand. "Two-fifty," he said finally.

"Maybe we could tell him the watch was stolen," Constance whispered to Toby. "If he's a true gentleman, he'll —"

Toby put a finger to his lips. "Shhh," he said. "Listen."

"I'll be back later this afternoon," the man was saying. "I have a bit of business to do just outside of town. I'd like you to give the watch a shine and wrap it up in paper. It's a present for my brother."

The shopkeeper nodded. "As you wish, sir. The watch will be ready."

The man in the top hat leaned across the counter. "Tell me, do you know of any folks around these parts

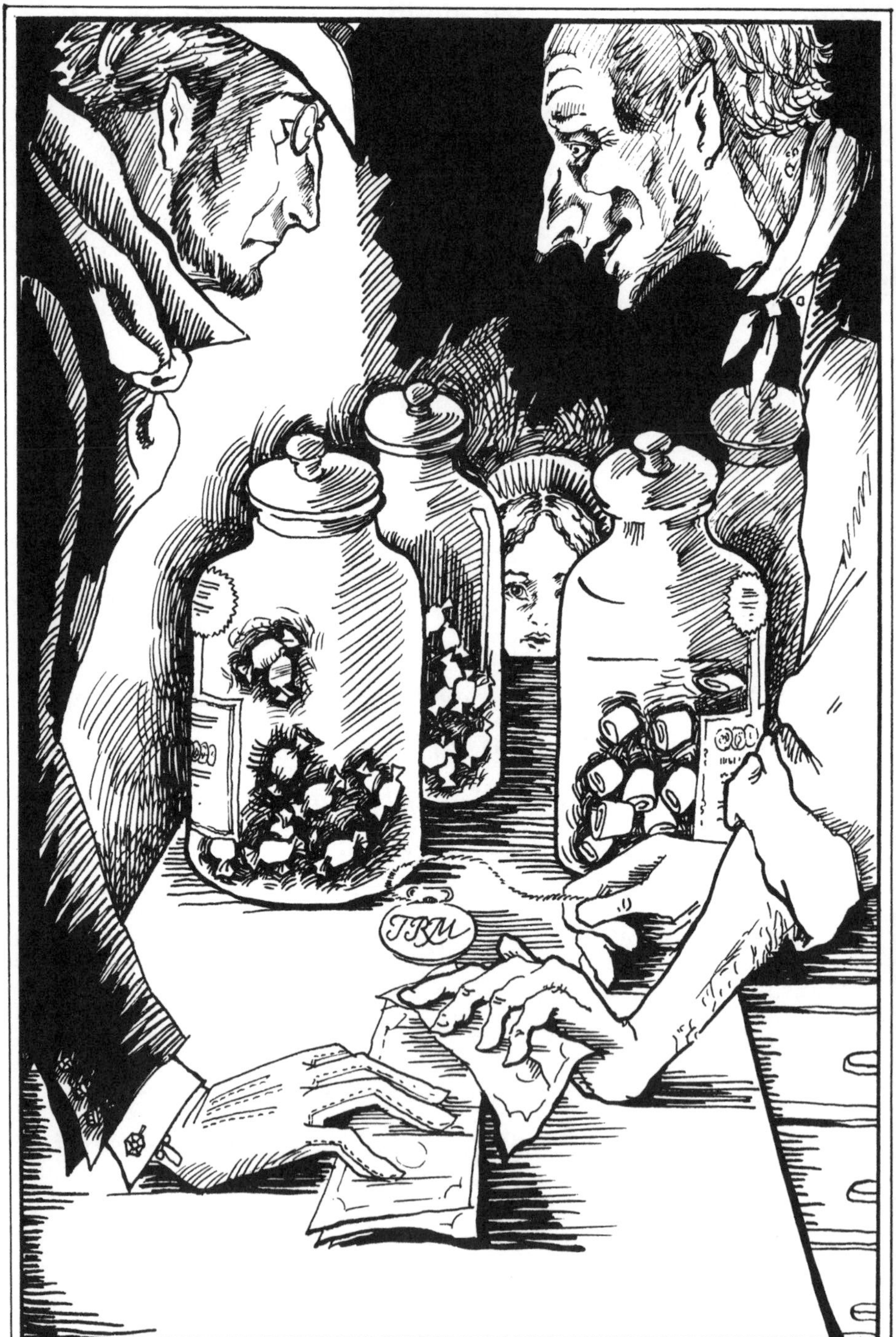
TRM

who are looking to sell a few trustworthy slaves? It's house slaves I'm looking for, in particular. My wife just lost her favorite woman to the consumption."

The shopkeeper shook his head. "No, sir, I don't know of anyone offhand. We just had a slave auction here in town a week or so ago."

The customer nodded. "Well, I did hear of someone a few miles outside of town who has a good woman he may be willing to sell. Morgan is his name, I believe. I'm on my way to see him right now." With a tip of his hat, he strode out the door.

Morgan! Constance felt herself beginning to panic. What if Uncle Tobias agreed to sell Hattie and Ezra before she and Toby could tell him about the watch?

She nudged her cousin. Toby's face had turned a peculiar shade of green. "What should we do now?" she whispered urgently.

"We'll just go after that man in the top hat and tell him my father's slaves aren't for sale," Toby said, his words spilling out in a nervous rush. "Then we could explain about the watch, and —"

"He's never going to believe us," Constance said impatiently. "Besides, we don't have any time to lose. We have to speak to your father before Mr. Top Hat does — or Hattie and Ezra may be sold off the plantation this very afternoon!"

10

Constance and Toby rushed out of the shop. The gentleman in the top hat had just stepped into his fancy black carriage. Constance and Toby watched glumly as the carriage rolled off down the street.

Constance groaned. "Now what?" she said.

"Father said he'd wait until this evening before he did anything," Toby pointed out. "He gave his word."

"Maybe so," Constance said. "But I still think we should go straight back to the plantation, just in case, and tell your father the whole story."

"I don't know if I can," Toby said, hanging his head. "I'm scared of what Father will do."

"It's always better to tell the truth," Constance said gently.

Toby didn't answer right away. "I reckon you're right," he said finally. "I sure don't want Hattie and Ezra sent away on account of me. I was only trying to help in the first place and everything got all mixed up."

Constance looked at him in surprise. "What do

you mean?"

Toby sighed. "Well, I happened to hear Hattie's husband, John, talking to another one of the field hands near the drying shed. John said he was fixing to take off for freedom up north. He was planning to come back for Hattie and Ezra. I thought maybe if he had a good sum of money to start, he could get set up sooner, and..." His voice trailed away.

"So you stole your father's watch and sold it, then gave the money to Ezra?" Constance prompted.

"That's right," Toby said. "Only Ezra didn't know what it was. I tucked the packet of money inside his shirt as I was going into the dining room and told him it was a present for his mama. I made him promise not to say anything to anyone, and he didn't."

"But what about Hattie?" Constance asked. "Wouldn't she have wondered how Ezra got all that money?"

Toby took a deep breath. "I told Hattie what I did, right after dinner. I wanted her and John and Ezra to have the money so they could start a new life up north real soon. But Hattie said she wouldn't have taken it, anyway; that it wasn't right."

"And she hasn't told your father she knows who really stole his watch?" Constance asked, frowning. "Even though she and Ezra might be sent away because of what you did?"

Toby nodded. "It was a foolish plan, I know. I should have realized that Hattie was too honest to take that money."

"Well, now you have even more reason to tell your father the truth," Constance said.

"I know," Toby said miserably.

Just then, the bells from a nearby church tower began to chime the hour.

Constance looked up at the old clock. "Oh!" she cried. "I'm supposed to be in front of the depot right about now. And it's a good thing, too, because it may be our only chance to catch up with Mr. Top Hat."

Toby looked puzzled. "The depot?" he said. "You aren't going to run away and leave us, are you? Why, you just got here."

"Of course not, Toby." Constance waved impatiently. "How did you get here this morning? Do you have a horse tied somewhere?"

"No," Toby said. "I got a ride in with one of our neighbors."

"Then we'll have to hurry," Constance said. "Let's go!" Constance picked up her skirt and began to run toward the depot. Toby was right behind her.

As they drew closer, Constance saw that a large, noisy crowd had begun to gather not far from the train tracks. *We'll never find Peter's cart now,* she thought. *And what were all of those men hooting and shouting about? Perhaps they were giving more speeches.*

Suddenly, a carriage drew up beside Constance and Toby. "Hullo there!" a voice called.

Constance shielded her eyes from the dust.

"Father!" she heard Toby say in surprise.

"Get in, both of you," Uncle Tobias ordered as the carriage came to a stop. "There's going to be trouble behind us."

Toby quickly helped Constance into the carriage and stepped up after her. "What's wrong, Father?" he asked as he and Constance settled onto the red leather seats.

Uncle Tobias looked grave. "It's that mob back there," he said. "A regiment of Mr. Lincoln's Yankee soldiers — the Sixth Massachusetts, they say — is marching across town toward the depot. They're on their way to Washington to defend the capital, and some of our Maryland boys are looking to stop them."

The shouts from the crowd began to grow louder. Constance hunched over in her seat and covered her ears.

Toby craned his neck to see out the window. "I can see the soldiers!" he said excitedly. Just then shots rang out, and his eyes grew wide in horror. "The people are shooting and throwing stones at them."

"Faster!" Uncle Tobias commanded the driver sharply.

Constance felt her pulse pounding in her temples. She'd never been so frightened in her whole life.

"There, now, Constance," Uncle Tobias said kindly, patting her on the knee. "We're quite safe in the carriage. There's nothing to worry about."

"But what about all those poor soldiers?" Constance asked.

Her uncle's lips tightened. "Well, my dear, war is a nasty business. And now it's become clear that it is unavoidable." He played with a pearl button on one of his kid gloves. "I'm a loyal Southerner, Maryland born and bred. But unlike most of my neighbors, I was hoping that a miracle would happen and President Lincoln would be able to hold the Union together."

There was a long silence as the carriage rattled on. Constance finally lifted her head and saw that they were surrounded by farm land and tobacco fields. She sighed in relief.

Then Uncle Tobias said, "What troubles me even more is knowing that Wood is somewhere in that crowd of hooligans. This morning he informed me that he's off to join the Confederate Army. I'm afraid there's nothing I can do to stop him this time."

Uncle Tobias gave Toby a sad smile. "It looks as though you'll be the new young master of the house, with your brother gone."

Constance saw Toby take a deep breath. Then he straightened his shoulders and said, "I have something to tell you, Father."

Uncle Tobias raised his bushy red brows. "I hope you're not planning to run off, too," he frowned. "What were you children doing in the city by yourselves?"

Toby glanced at Constance, then turned to meet

his father's gaze. "It all had to do with your watch, sir."

Constance drew back against the leather seat as Toby told his father the whole story. The only part he left out was about John planning to escape. Instead he said that he was hoping that Hattie and her family might make a break for freedom. When Toby had finished, Constance saw a dark shadow pass across her uncle's face.

"I'm disappointed in you, son," he said. "Taking that watch was very wrong, and selling it was inexcusable. You may have thought your intentions were honorable, though as you imagine, I do not agree with them." He paused. "However, you have further disgraced yourself as a Morgan and as a gentleman by not telling the truth. Innocent people very close to you could have been wrongly punished."

"I know, Father," Toby whispered. "And I am very sorry."

Uncle Tobias nodded curtly. "I will deal with you later, you may be sure. But I don't see any reason to disturb your mother with all of this. She's upset enough about Wood. We'll take the carriage in the back way."

"What about Hattie and Ezra?" Toby asked anxiously. "You won't sell them off the plantation now, will you?"

"No," Uncle Tobias said. "I will send your Mr. Top Hat on his way. But I believe you will have something to say to Hattie and Ezra about this unpleasant matter."

"Yes, Father," Toby said. "I will tell them how very sorry I am."

Uncle Tobias turned to Constance. "Are you still willing to stay with us, my dear? Even after all of this unpleasantness?"

He sounds so worried, Constance thought. *He must truly care about me, after all, even if I am a Yankee.* Then she glanced over at her cousin. Toby was looking back at her with hopeful eyes. She did like all of the Morgans, except perhaps for Melanie. But Melanie had surprised her at dinner that afternoon. Perhaps there was still a small chance that the two of them would be friends someday. "I would be very pleased to stay," she said. And she did feel pleased. It felt good to be part of a family.

When they arrived at the plantation a few minutes later, Rachel told them in hushed tones that Aunt Georgina had asked not to be disturbed. Toby followed Uncle Tobias into the library with Hattie and Ezra. Constance started up the stairs, eager for once to go to her room.

As she walked toward her door, she heard muffled sobs from behind the closed doors of the next room.

Melanie, Constance told herself, frowning. *Should she go in?*

The sobs grew louder. Timidly, Constance knocked on the door and walked inside. "Melanie?"

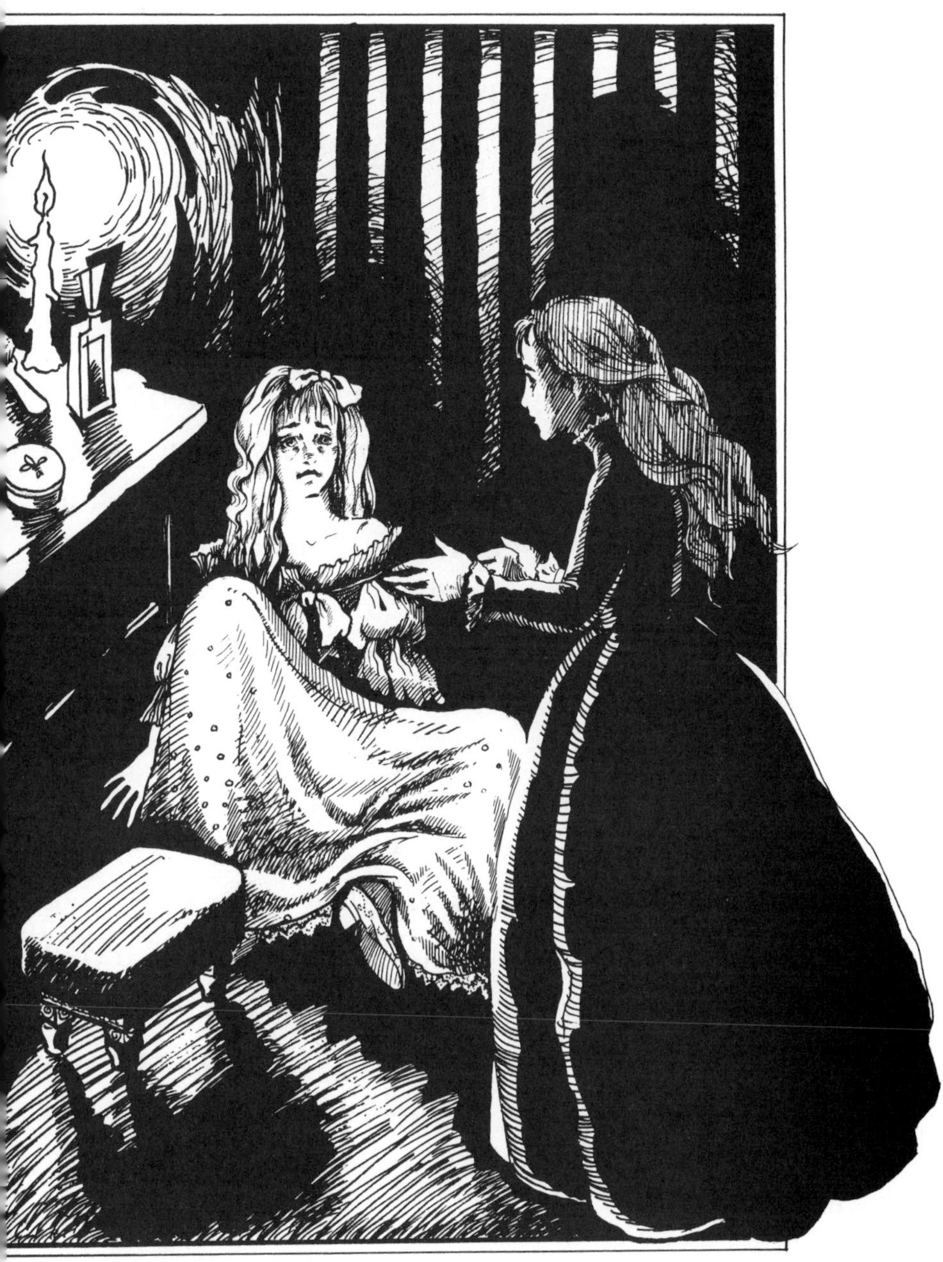

she called softly. Her cousin was sitting on the floor in her silk dress, her head down on an embroidered footstool.

The sobs suddenly stopped. Then Melanie raised her tear-stained face. "Wood is gone," she said in a shaky voice. "He went off and left us all alone. He may never come back home."

"No!" Constance said, rushing forward to put her arms around her cousin. "Don't say that, Melanie."

"It's true," Melanie said, sniffling. "I wanted him to be a brave, handsome Confederate soldier. But I never thought about what might really happen." She covered her face with her hands, burying her head in Constance's shoulder.

"Everything will be fine," Constance said gently. "Before you know it, Wood will come marching right back."

Melanie dropped her hands and looked at Constance. Her eyes were red and puffy. "Do you really think so, Cousin Constance?"

Constance hesitated. "Of course," she said, trying hard to smile. "Why, this nasty old war will be over in no time."

"I hope you're right," Melanie said quietly.

I hope so, too, Constance thought. But she truly wasn't sure.